AFTER DARK
A VAMPS NOVEL

AFTER DARK
A VAMPS NOVEL

NANCY A. COLLINS

HARPER TEEN

AN IMPRINT OF HARPERCOLLINS*PUBLISHERS*

HarperTeen is an imprint of HarperCollins Publishers.

Vamps: After Dark
Copyright © 2009 by Nancy A. Collins

Library of Congress Cataloging-in-Publication Data
Collins, Nancy A.
   After dark / Nancy A. Collins. — 1st ed.
      p.   cm. — (Vamps ; #3)
   Summary: Vampire half sisters and archrivals Cally and
Lilith pursue high-stakes careers and even higher-stakes romance
in the glamorous world of New York's vampire elite.
   ISBN 978-0-06-134919-5
   [1. Vampires—Fiction.   2.   Sisters—Fiction.   3.   Social
classes—Fiction.   4. Wealth—Fiction.   5. New York (N.Y.)—
Fiction.]   I. Title.
PZ7.C683528Af   2009   2008027470
[Fic]—dc22   CIP
                                                      AC

Typography by Andrea Vandergrift
09 10 11 12 13   CG/RRDH   10 9 8 7 6 5 4 3 2

❖

First Edition

In loving memory of Scrapple 1994–2008
"Mama's Little Stinker"

Rarely do great beauty and great virtue dwell together.
—Petrarch, *De Remedies*

CHAPTER 1

Cally had been to Rauhnacht parties before, but none as elaborate as this. The difference between how the New Bloods and Old Bloods celebrated the arrival of the Dark Season was the difference between a children's Halloween party and the Carnival of Venice. Now that the opening waltz of the evening was over, the debutantes and their escorts were receiving congratulations from their parents' friends and associates. Everywhere she looked, gorgeous women in glittering designer evening gowns and men in elegant dress mingled. The air was alive with laughter, live music, and the ring of fine crystal as the revelers toasted one another.

At the center of the ballroom was a huge fountain fashioned of hammered gold offering an endless supply of O positive blood. As Count Orlock's guests milled about, chatting and laughing among themselves, they were free to fill their glasses from any of its fancy spigots. A small army of Orlock servants wearing classic footman gear also carried platters laden with wineglasses for those revelers who thirsted for less-common blood types.

The floor was open to whoever wished to dance the night away. Dozens of couples swirled about, moving in perfect time.

As the only daughter of a single mother, Cally had grown up far removed from the glitz and glamour of the jet-setting Old Bloods. Then, after sixteen years of anonymity, her biological father had suddenly taken an interest in her. The immediate transition from a low-rent New Blood high school to Bathory Academy had been jarring. Cally's problem wasn't the challenge of adapting to a new life of privilege and financial security—she was pretty sure she could figure that one out. She was more troubled by the fact that she had just been introduced to all of Old Blood society (at least those who mattered) under false pretenses.

Although Baron Karl Metzger claimed her as his daughter, Cally's biological father was really Victor Todd, one of the world's richest vampires and Baron Metzger's lord and master. However, since Victor knew his wife, Irina, and his daughter Lilith would take a dim view of any pretender to the Todd bloodright, it was necessary for Cally to masquerade as another man's child if she wanted to stay alive. The fact that Lilith knew the truth and was using it to blackmail Victor didn't exactly make things easier. And as if that weren't dicey enough, there was also the problem of Cally's mother being a human.

"My dear, there's someone here I want you to meet."

Cally glanced up at Baron Metzger. "Who is it?"

"Just a friend of mine. Ah, there she is!" he said, pointing in the direction of a woman dressed in a midnight-blue silk crepe gown with matching lambskin opera gloves.

"Karl! By the Founders, it's good to see you!" the woman said as she clasped Metzger's hands, ritualistically kissing the air to either side of his cheeks. Her sleek, black hair was worn in a Cleopatra bob.

"You look fabulous as ever, darling!" Baron Metzger smiled. "I would like you to meet my daughter. Cally, this is my old friend—"

"Uh-uh-uh!" the woman said, wagging a finger in admonishment. "You *know* you're not allowed to say the *O* word around me!"

"Excuse me, *liebchen*, I forgot!" Metzger chuckled. "Make that my very *dear* friend Sister Midnight."

"Not *the* Sister Midnight?" Cally gasped in surprise.

Sister Midnight was the owner of the most exclusive vampire-only boutique in New York City, with equally successful branches in Beverly Hills, London, Paris, Moscow, and Tokyo. If Victor Todd was the vampire world's equivalent of Bill Gates, Sister Midnight was its Martha Stewart.

"One and the same, I'm afraid," she replied. "It's nice to know my reputation precedes me, even among the younger generation."

"It's an honor to meet you, ma'am!"

"She *is* a lovely little thing, Karl!" Sister Midnight said, obviously pleased. "Where have you been hiding her all this time? I had no idea you had a daughter until I saw you coming down the stairs."

"Cally's mother was one of my concubines," Metzger replied matter-of-factly. "Now that my dear wife, Adela, is no more, I am free to formally claim Cally as part of my family."

Sister Midnight nodded her understanding, seeming to accept his explanation without batting an eye. "I can tell she's inherited your fashion sense! I absolutely *love* that gown you have on, my child! Where did you get it? Who's the designer?"

"Well, I, uh . . ." Although she was flattered by the praise, Cally was hesitant to admit what she was wearing was homemade.

"Come, now—there's no point in being modest!"

Baron Metzger said proudly. "She designed the gown on her own!"

Sister Midnight's jaw dropped in surprise. "Cally, is your father telling me the truth?"

"Yes," she replied, blushing. "I made it myself."

"Do you have any more 'originals'?"

"Yes, but most of them are packed away right now. . . ." Cally caught herself before she could say any more. The moment the Grand Ball was over, she was headed to JFK International Airport, where her father had a private jet fueled and ready to fly her to Europe. No one was supposed to know she was leaving, especially Lilith, so she had to be extra careful about what she said during the course of the night.

Although she didn't want to leave New York, she had agreed to the relocation out of concern for her mother's safety and a desire to please her father. But she sensed that Victor's sudden interest in her welfare had more to do with her having inherited a rare supernatural genetic trait known as the Shadow Hand than actual affection.

Sister Midnight reached into her satin purse, took out a business card, and handed it to Cally. "Come by the boutique in a couple of days. Bring along a few samples of your work. If I like what I see, perhaps we can make an arrangement for something later on?"

Cally blinked in disbelief. "Are you serious?"

"I'm *never* serious," Sister Midnight said with a throaty laugh. "But I *do* mean what I say!" She turned and waved at someone across the room. "I'd love to chat, darling, but I just saw someone that I simply *must* talk to!"

Cally stared in awe at the business card. "I can't believe that just happened," she told the Baron. "I've always dreamed of getting a chance like this—but I never thought it would happen. It's too bad I'm not in a position to take advantage of the situation."

"Don't let such things dampen your spirits, my dear. From here on, you'll have plenty of opportunities," the Baron said reassuringly. "Now that you are one of us, doors that were once closed are open. All you have to do is walk through them."

As Cally mulled over Metzger's words, Melinda Mauvais emerged from the crowd of expensively dressed partygoers.

"There you are!" Melinda said, heaving a sigh of relief. "I've been looking all over for you!"

"Who is this charming young lady?" Metzger asked, eyeing the other girl's chic Valentino gown.

"Baron—I mean Dad," Cally said, quickly correcting herself, "I'd like to introduce you to my good friend Melinda."

"Pleased to meet you, sir," Melinda said, offering him her hand.

Baron Metzger clicked his heels as he bowed at the waist. "The pleasure is all mine."

"I'd like to borrow your daughter for a few minutes, Baron," Melinda said, taking Cally by the arm. "My parents would like to meet her."

Anton Mauvais was a handsome man with a slightly puffy, fretful face, who appeared to be in his late thirties. Standing beside him was his wife, Layla, a slender, stunningly beautiful woman with skin the color of mahogany. She was dressed in a backless gold lamé evening gown and she wore her hair close to her skull, dramatically highlighting her catlike black eyes.

"Mother? Father? I'd like you to meet my friend Cally Monture."

"You're the half-blood, am I right?" Anton Mauvais asked, his voice as blunt as a hammer.

"*Dad!*" Melinda groaned in embarrassment.

"There's no need to be *rude*, Anton!" Layla said reproachfully.

"I'm *not* being rude, just truthful!" Mauvais snapped defensively. "The girl's mother is a New Blood, is she not?"

Layla sighed wearily. "For once, I would like to go somewhere without you bringing caste into the conversation!"

Unsure how she should react, Cally was surprised to find her surrogate father suddenly at her elbow.

"Good evening, Anton," Baron Metzger said flatly. "Congratulations on the debut of your lovely daughter."

"Thank you, Karl. Congratulations to you as well. I was just asking your girl here a couple of questions about—"

"Yes, I know what you were doing," Metzger said, cutting Mauvais off in mid-sentence. "She has been properly introduced to Old Blood society as my daughter. Should you have any further questions, ask them of me."

"For someone who so proudly paraded his bastard for all to see, you seem to resent the term 'New Blood,'" Mauvais said with a sneer.

"Save it for your fellow Purists," Metzger replied coldly. "They have time for such drivel; I don't."

Mauvais's face contorted, and for the space of a heartbeat, he became a snarling wolf from the neck up, fangs bared, eyes flashing with a murderous fire.

"Anton!"

Layla's voice was like the crack of a whip. Mauvais's wolf head disappeared as swiftly as it had materialized. He scowled at his wife but quickly averted his gaze on seeing her anger.

"I'm going to go freshen my drink," he said sullenly.

Layla Mauvais placed a hand on Metzger's arm. "I'm *so* terribly sorry about all that, Baron. Ever since Anton joined Count de Laval's retinue as an adviser, he's been insufferable! Purist this, Purist that!" She took a deep breath, forcing a smile onto her face. "But enough about my husband! So, Cally, you are the one who saved my daughter's life? I owe you a great debt." Layla threw her arms around Cally in an unexpected embrace. "You have a *very* brave daughter, Baron!"

"Is that so?" Metzger said, raising an eyebrow.

"Did she not tell you? She saved my Melinda from Van Helsings."

Metzger's surprise gave way to alarm. "She did *what*?"

"We were clubbing," Melinda explained. "There was an ambush. We would have been staked if it hadn't been for Cally. She killed all three of them using her stormgathering ability."

Metzger turned to stare at Cally. "You killed *three* Van Helsings? All by yourself?"

"Kinda," Cally replied uncomfortably.

The truth was, she hadn't killed three Van Helsings on the pier that night. She hadn't even killed two. Melinda herself had slain one of the vampire hunters, while she used her ability to control lightning to incapacitate the second. As for the third . . . well, the less said about him, the better.

"Brave *and* modest," Layla Mauvais said admiringly. "My Melinda is *very* lucky to have a friend like you, my dear! Just as you are lucky to have such a fine father."

"Yes, I guess I am." Cally smiled and glanced across the room at Victor Todd, who was being congratulated on his daughter's debut. As she watched, Victor put a fatherly arm around Lilith's shoulders. The smile slipped from Cally's face and she quickly looked away.

"Good evening, Mr. and Mrs. Todd."

"Good evening, Jules." Irina smiled. "You're looking *very* handsome tonight."

"And you look as splendid as ever, madam," he replied, kissing Irina's hand. "My father wishes to congratulate Lilith."

"Of course, my dear boy!" Victor said, smiling indulgently. "Please take her to him!"

Lilith leaned over and whispered into her father's ear, "Why can't Count de Laval come over here and congratulate me himself? Why do *I* have to go to *him*?"

"Because he may very well be the next Lord Chamberlain, that's why," Victor growled back under his breath.

Lilith rolled her eyes and sighed, just to make her feelings clear. The moment they were safely out of earshot, Jules roughly grabbed her arm.

"What in the name of the Founders are you trying to pull?" he asked angrily.

"What do you mean?"

"I'm talking about Xander!" Jules snapped. "Why did you pick *him* to be your escort?"

"You're one to talk!" she replied heatedly. "You *know* how much I hate Cally, and you didn't even have the decency to tell me you're her escort for the ball."

"That's different."

"How so?"

Jules paused for a second as he tried to come up with a reason. When he couldn't, he became angrier, as if that somehow proved his point. "It just *is*! Besides, we're not bound yet. And even if we *were*, it's not your place to tell me what to do."

Lilith was about to tell Jules she knew about his affair with her now ex-friend Carmen Duivel but stopped when she realized she was standing in front of his father. Count Julian de Laval was an elegant man who looked like an older, jaded version of his son.

"Good evening, Your Excellency," Lilith said, curtsying. "You wished to speak to me?"

"Indeed we do, my dear," Count de Laval replied languidly. "We wish to confer our congratulations upon your introduction to the Old Blood."

"I'm honored, Count de Laval."

"We would also like to thank you for appointing our nephew as your escort."

"Since your son could not serve in that capacity,"

Lilith lied, shooting a sharp look at Jules, "I decided his closest male relative would be the next-best thing. Xander is an excellent dancer, by the way."

"In that, at least, he resembles his mother's side of the family." Count de Laval looked Lilith up and down, taking in her long blond hair, sparkling blue eyes, and Marchesa gown. "Your dress highlights your figure wonderfully, my dear. If there is one problem with women of our caste, it's that they have narrow hips. You, on the other hand, have very nice, *wide* hips. That will help during pregnancies."

Lilith had to bite her tongue to keep the outrage inside her from spewing forth in a torrent of choice obscenities. Who did he think he was? More importantly, who did he think *she* was? Some peasant girl brought in to freshen up the bloodline? New stock so his grandchildren wouldn't end up bat boys? As she turned away, Jules followed her.

"Why didn't you tell me that's why you picked Xander?"

"Like you said: we're not bound yet. I don't have to explain myself to anyone, let alone you. Don't bother taking me back to my parents—I can make it on my own."

"So—what did Count de Laval have to say?" Irina asked eagerly, pouncing on her returning daughter like a hungry cat on a mouse. Besides crosswords and sudoku, one of her favorite hobbies was puzzling out the hidden meanings buried within the idle chitchat of others.

"You mean other than him making it clear he views me as nothing more than a broodmare?" Lilith replied, her voice quavering in outrage. "He looked at me like I was something he scraped off his shoe!"

"Did he say anything about me or your father?"

"No, he didn't. And even if he had—so what? It would mean as much as if he'd talked about his valet—possibly even less!"

"Keep your voice down! We're in public!" Victor snapped, flashing his displeasure. "Count de Laval is ethnarch of the descendants of Faroch the Enslaver—he can look down his nose at us all he wants! At least for now, that is. Once you and Jules are formally bound, it'll be a different story."

"Daddy, I really, really *don't* like Count de Laval! And to be honest, I'm seriously thinking about breaking up with Jules! If it was up to me—"

"But it's *not* up to you!" Irina hissed, grabbing Lilith's wrist hard enough to make her wince. She had long ago learned the art of inflicting pain on her daughter while outwardly appearing to be a doting mother. "As for Jules, you don't *have* to love him or even tolerate his company—just marry him and bear his offspring:

that is *all*. And that's exactly what you're going to do, young lady! Because I'm *not* going to let you get in the way of my very own palace on the Côte d'Azur, you understand?"

"Perfectly," Lilith said as she massaged the quickly fading bruises on her wrist.

CHAPTER 2

Carmen Duivel smiled wanly as her escort, Sergei Savanovic, handed her a champagne flute full of blood. Sergei frowned. Normally Carmen was the life of the party. He'd never seen her so subdued before.

"What's wrong? I thought you'd be whooping it up with Lilith and the others. Why are you sitting on the sidelines, watching everyone else party?"

Carmen heaved a deep sigh, and for a moment it seemed like she might cry. "I know I should be out there having a good time, Sergei, but this has turned into the worst night of my life—ever!"

"It can't be as bad as all that."

"Just before midnight, while we were in the waiting room upstairs, things kind of got out of hand between

Lilith and Cally. I ended up saying some things I shouldn't have and, well, Lilith found out about me and Jules."

"I stand corrected: that *is* bad!" As Jules's best friend, Sergei had known about the affair from the start. He had his own opinion about why Carmen was sleeping around with Jules, but he knew enough to keep his trap shut.

"Now I'm afraid Lilith is going to tell Oliver."

"So what if she does?" Sergei shrugged. "It's not like you're promised to each other."

"It's just that whenever Ollie feels like he's been slighted, he goes into these awful tantrums!"

"I've never cared for the guy," Sergei said bluntly. "No offense, but I've never understood why you hang with that jerk."

"My mom thinks we make a good-looking couple." Carmen gestured at her mother, Camille Duivel, who was busy hobnobbing with some of the members of her country club. "She says that makes it easier to get into hot nightclubs and attract prey. Which is true, I guess. But Oliver treats me kind of mean. That's why I started fooling around with Jules in the first place. Now Jules treats me just like Ollie does. No one ever appreciates me."

"Well, *I* appreciate you," Sergei said, patting her hand.

* * *

As Cally watched the stylishly dressed partygoers swirl around the floor to the strains of *Die Fledermaus*, she found herself thinking of Peter. Because her father was a vampire and his father was a vampire hunter, it had been impossible for them to enjoy the pleasures young lovers take for granted, such as going dancing. Although she was the one who'd insisted on breaking up, she still had strong feelings for him. Indeed, while waltzing with Jules earlier that night, she had even imagined Peter's face, pale and distraught, pressed against one of the windows that looked out onto the gardens.

Although she would miss her friends, Cally was beginning to think that perhaps moving to Europe wasn't such a bad idea after all. Clearly she needed the space in order to get over Peter—and she was certain it would help him get over her, too.

Being in the same city made it far too tempting to try to reestablish contact. And the more time they spent together, the greater the risk. Not even her father's status could protect her if it was discovered that she had been intimate with a descendant of Pieter Van Helsing, legendary scourge of the vampire race.

Cally suddenly became aware that she was rubbing the palm of her left hand against her thigh and forced herself to stop. She had been experiencing an odd, intermittent prickling sensation in her hand throughout the evening.

It must be nerves, she told herself.

Hearing a polite cough at her elbow, Cally turned to find Faustus "Lucky" Maledetto standing beside her. Lucky was the older brother of her good friends Bella and Bette. He looked especially yummy tonight in a double-breasted tux with wide lapels. Cally couldn't deny his charm, but her attraction to Lucky was tempered by the knowledge that he was the son of her father's sworn enemy, Vincent Maledetto, leader of the Strega crime cartel. Victor had already warned her about being friendly with members of the Maledetto family; although she had recently decided to ignore his wishes when it came to the twins, openly socializing with their brother was another thing entirely.

"May I have this dance?"

"Aren't you supposed to be escorting Melinda Mauvais?"

"Jules de Laval is supposed to be your escort for the evening, isn't he? But I don't see him nearby," Lucky pointed out.

Cally looked around the crowded ballroom and felt a twinge of jealousy as she spotted her father exchanging pleasantries with yet another group of associates who had come to congratulate him on Lilith's debut.

As she watched her father's friends fawn over the acknowledged heiress to the Todd fortune, Cally thought: *What harm could dancing with Lucky Maledetto possibly do? So what if Victor doesn't approve? I'm leaving New York City for good, aren't I? In the end, it won't make a blood drop's difference. He'll get over it.*

"Okay." She smiled, nodding. "But just *one* dance."

"Just one," he promised, taking her hand in his as they swung out onto the dance floor. Cally was impressed by how smoothly he moved. He really was quite a dancer.

"Is something on your mind?" Lucky asked as he drew her close. "You seem a little preoccupied."

"I'm sorry," she apologized. "I'm just going through some complicated stuff in my life right now."

"Anything I could help you with?"

Cally looked up into his eyes, impressed by how self-assured he was. She had no doubt there were few problems Lucky Maledetto could not resolve if he put his mind to it. "It's sweet of you to ask, but I don't think so. Besides, you've done enough for me already."

"You mean scaring off Johnny Muerto and his gang?" Lucky chuckled as they turned. "Scum like Muerto need to be taught their place. And I'm happy to teach it to them." He cocked his head to one side, studying Cally's short dark hair and pixielike face. "Do you know what the snowman said to the other snowman?"

Cally blinked, unsure of what to make of the question. "No . . . what did he say?"

"'Do you smell a carrot?'"

"Ohhh! That was *awful!*" Cally groaned, laughing despite herself.

"See?" Lucky smiled, holding her gently. "I knew I could help."

Boris Orlock, master of King's Stone, rose from his throne of carved bone and ivory. He tapped his crystal wineglass with a long, curving nail, causing it to chime like a bell. The musicians set aside their instruments, and the babble of voices that filled the ballroom quickly subsided. Everyone turned to face their host. A tall, imposing figure of breathtaking ugliness, Count Orlock stood before his elegantly coiffed and haute-coutured guests like a phantom at the feast.

"Everyone, please lift your glasses!" he commanded.

Count Orlock hoisted his glass high, his baritone voice rolling across the room like thunder.

"I would like to take this time to propose a toast! To the beautiful young women who have debuted here tonight: may your futures be as lovely as yourselves! In the name of the Founders: live long and drink deep!"

"*So say we all!*" the crowd replied, their voices melding as one.

* * *

When Cally brought her goblet to her lips, she heard the sound of breaking glass from somewhere behind her. As she turned in the direction of the sound, thinking perhaps a waiter had dropped a serving tray, the windows facing the garden suddenly shattered inward. What looked like cans of shaving cream flew through the ballroom, landing on the polished floor. As one came to rest near her foot, Cally realized that's not what they were.

They were tear-gas canisters.

"Get back!" Lucky yelled, pushing Cally behind him as a dense, grayish cloud erupted into the air. "Cover your mouth!"

Within seconds the ballroom became a scene of mass chaos, the music and laughter replaced by screams. Cally was buffeted back and forth as the guests crashed into one another trying to escape the rapidly spreading fumes. Her eyes swimming with tears, she reached out, groping blindly through the wall of smoke.

"Lucky! Where are you?"

"I'm here! Don't worry—I've got you!" he shouted, his strong hands closing around her own.

Suddenly the crowd surrounding her began to surge in the opposite direction. Cally tried to move toward Lucky, only to be wrenched from his grasp. Barely able to see and breathe, she was borne away by a living tide. Somewhere in the madness, she could hear

Baron Metzger calling her name, but she could not see him, much less tell which direction his voice was coming from.

At first Lilith thought the explosions and gouts of smoke were some kind of pyrotechnic display Count Orlock had arranged for the amusement of his guests. But when her eyes started burning and her mascara began to run, she realized the fireworks had nothing to do with the Grand Ball.

"Daddy—what's going on?" she wailed.

Victor Todd took a monogrammed silk handkerchief from the breast pocket of his tuxedo and covered his nose and mouth. "We're under attack, princess!"

"Van Helsings? *Here?* They must be mad!" Irina coughed.

"Get Lilith out of here *now*," Victor said, pushing her toward her mother.

"You heard your father," Irina said, grabbing her daughter's arm. "We've got to get out of this place!"

"Where's Jules?" Lilith looked around, but her eyes were stinging too much from the acrid smoke for her to see more than a few feet in any direction.

"The de Lavals can take care of themselves!" Irina snapped. "We've got to escape!"

"Don't tell me what to do!" Lilith said, pulling away from her mother.

"Lilith! Come back here!"

Ignoring her mother, Lilith pushed her way through the crowd. After only a few steps she quickly found herself trapped, unable to move forward or go back. As the choking fumes burned her eyes and mouth, she was overwhelmed by the urgent need to free herself from the crushing press.

"Get out of my way, damn you! I've got to get out!" she screamed, kicking and clawing at those closest to her. Those on the receiving end of Lilith's slashing nails began doing the same to those ahead of them, triggering a chain reaction.

There was a sound of smashing glass and splintering wood, immediately followed by the smell of sea air from the nearby Atlantic as the panicked partygoers pushed their way through the French doors, spilling out onto the garden terrace like hornets from a burning hive.

Finally out of the tear gas, Cally staggered across the stone terrace toward the wide, curving stairs that led to the gardens below.

"Fire!"

Cally looked up just in time to see dozens of crossbow arrows flying toward the terrace. She ducked, putting a marble replica of the *Venus de Milo* between her and the deadly rain. As she watched from her hiding place, she saw one of the other guests jump atop the balustrade's railing, instantly shapeshifting into his winged form.

With a beat of his eight-foot wings, the transformed vampire shot up into the night sky in a desperate attempt to escape the Van Helsings' crossbows before they could reload. At first it looked like he had succeeded, but then a shadow soared from the roofline of the building.

With just a few beats of its own leathery wings, the gargoyle easily overtook the fleeing vampire, who screamed as the beast's slashing talons destroyed his right wing. Unable to maintain balance, the vampire spun out of control and crashed a hundred feet down into the hedges that ringed the gardens.

Cally's guts tightened as she listened to the gargoyle shriek in triumph. Things had just gotten a whole lot worse: both the Van Helsings and their pet were out for blood.

Lilith pushed her way out onto the terrace, literally climbing over her fellow guests to escape the smoke-filled confines of the ballroom. With her gown in tatters and black tears streaking her face, she no longer looked like the vampire debutante who had held every eye in the room.

"Jules! Mom! Daddy! Where are you?" she cried out, hoping to spot a familiar face in the surrounding crowd.

"Lilith! Look out!"

Lilith turned to find the last person in the world she wanted to see, Cally Monture, cowering behind a statue, pointing at something in the sky. She heard the sound of wings—*big wings*—coming up from behind her. Lilith spun around to see something that looked like a cross between a pit bull and a crocodile bearing down on her, talons outstretched. She screamed as the gargoyle snatched her up in its claws and bore her into the night sky.

"Let go!" Lilith shrieked, struggling to free herself from the gargoyle's viselike grip. "Help! Help me!"

In response to her cry, something large and gray landed on the gargoyle's back and yanked on the loop of heavy chain encircling the beast's throat, turning the collar into a makeshift garrote.

Lilith thought she was being rescued by her father or Jules in winged form, but when she got a good look at the hideous creature riding the gargoyle's back, she wasn't sure if it had come to rescue her or was simply fighting for its share of the spoils.

The gargoyle snarled as it tried to unseat its unwanted passenger, but the mystery flier proved unshakable, hanging on to the chain around the beast's neck like a rodeo rider atop a raging bull. Roaring in pain and anger, the gargoyle let go of Lilith, sending her plummeting to the earth fifty feet below.

As the ground zoomed up to meet her, Lilith realized she had neither the time nor the skill to shapeshift into her winged form quickly enough to avoid being hurt. Even though a fall from such a height wouldn't kill a vampire, it would hurt a *whole lot*. And if she smashed her skull hard enough to damage her brain, the injuries could very well prove permanent, even with her near-instantaneous regenerative ability. All she could do was close her eyes and scream.

Just as she was about to smash into the marble paving stones of the terrace, a figure darted forward and caught her in its outstretched arms. Lilith spread the fingers covering her face to peep out at her savior, expecting to see Jules's handsome face.

"Exo?" Lilith gasped in amazement.

Xander Orlock, son of Count Boris Orlock, flashed a relieved smile as he put her back on her feet. He turned and shouted to his cousin, who was hurrying in their direction.

"Make sure Lilith gets to safety!"

"Sure thing, cuz!" Jules said, taking Lilith by the arm.

"What about you?" she asked, looking over her shoulder at Xander.

He pointed to where the gargoyle and the mystery flier fought in midair like a pair of sparring hawks. "I'm going to help Klaus take care of business." With that,

Xander transformed into his winged form and, with a single beat of his wings, flew up to join the battle raging overhead.

"Come on, Lili—you heard Exo," Jules said, dragging her back to the relative safety of the ballroom. "We've got to get out of here!"

"Who's Klaus?" Lilith asked as she watched Xander's hell-bat form strike the gargoyle from the other direction.

"That is." Jules pointed to the hideous creature battling the gargoyle. "He's Xander's older brother."

Cally watched in mute shock as Lilith was snatched up by the marauding gargoyle. She wasn't sure what she was more surprised by: a real, live gargoyle on the wing or the fact that her demi-sister's makeup and hair looked like shit.

As something swooped down from atop the north tower and tackled the gargoyle in midair, Cally was ready to leap out and block her sister's fall. Although she and Lilith had come close to killing each other on several occasions, Cally could not stand by and simply watch her get hurt, possibly even die.

After all, they shared blood, even if it was bad.

Before she could act, someone grabbed her by the arm and yanked her backward. A Van Helsing, his face covered by a gas mask, loomed over her. She had been so distracted by Lilith and the gargoyle that she hadn't noticed him sneaking up the garden stairs behind her.

She jerked her arm free and grabbed the vampire hunter by the neck, lifting him off the ground. His jackbooted feet kicked at the air as he clawed at the fingers tightening around his throat.

"Cally! It's me!" a muffled voice shouted from inside the gas mask.

"Peter?" Cally gasped, instantly relinquishing her hold. "Then I *wasn't* hallucinating!" she said as he peeled the gas mask away from his face. "You really *were* standing at the window! What is going on? Has your father lost his mind? Why is he taking on the Old Bloods like this?"

A look of anguish filled Peter Van Helsing's dark brown eyes. "I'm sorry, Cally—you have to believe that I *never* meant for things to get this out of hand!"

Cally wasn't sure what he meant, but she definitely didn't like the sound of it. "Peter, what did you *do*?"

"I told my father you were leaving for Europe after the Grand Ball," he admitted, avoiding her eyes. "He's determined to either capture you or kill you before you can leave the country."

Cally's confusion was quickly replaced by a slowly sinking dread. "But how would he even *know* where the ball was being held? I *never* told you that!"

"You dropped an RSVP envelope in the graveyard

that night you broke up with me. It had Orlock's name and address written on it. I gave it to him."

Cally, who had never been ill a day in her life, suddenly felt the need to throw up. "You mean this is all because of *me*?" she asked, gesturing to the carnage that surrounded them.

"I didn't want you to go away!" Peter said, grasping her hand. "I *love* you, Cally! I *need* you! I thought if my father captured you, then you'd have no choice *but* to stay with me! You have to understand!" he pleaded, searching her face for signs of forgiveness. "The moment I realized how dangerous my father's plan was, I tried to stop it. I called your cell phone to tell you to stay away, but it was too late—your mother said you were already gone. . . ."

"My mother? What *about* my mother?" Cally asked sharply, pulling away.

"I talked to her, that's all—she wasn't making much sense—I tried to warn her. I told her to escape."

"Peter, *why* would my mother need to escape?"

Peter spilled out his guilt. "They know where you live, Cally—they had someone following Todd and he led them right to you—I'm sorry, so sorry."

"Peter, what happened to my mother?" Cally's voice had become as hard and cold as steel.

"That doesn't matter right now; all that matters is getting you to safety!" Peter grabbed her. "I have to smuggle you out of here before my father's people get their hands on you."

"You're not taking me *anywhere!*" she said angrily as she wrenched herself free. "I'm not leaving my father and friends behind!"

"Please, Cally! You've got to trust me!"

Cally's eyes filled with tears. "*Trust you?* I *did* trust you—and *this* is what it got me! How could you betray me this way, Peter? How could you?"

Unable to stand being near the man she loved any longer, Cally turned and ran into the open, unmindful of the crossbow arrows whizzing through the air.

CHAPTER 3

As Carmen dodged the arrows raining down from the sky, someone stepped on the hem of her full-length gown, throwing her off balance. She tumbled headlong, coming to rest at the foot of the garden stairs. She cried out in pain and fear as she was trampled by her fellow Old Bloods. As she raised her head, one of the vampire hunters stepped out from behind a nearby bush and pointed his crossbow at her.

Before the Van Helsing could pull the trigger, a huge wolf with fur the color of coal leaped out of the shadows, sinking its bared fangs deep into the hunter's throat. A moment later Sergei Savanovic stood up, wiping the blood from his mouth. He grabbed Carmen by the hand, pulling her onto her feet.

"Come on—let's get out of here!"

Even though she was more scared than she'd ever been in her life, Carmen smiled.

"Lilith! Where are you? Princess!" Victor shouted, trying desperately to spot his daughter's honey-blond head among the confusion.

The damned Van Helsings knew their prey all too well. They had banked on the vampire's instinctual fear of fire and used the tear gas and smoke bombs to spark a panic. Only minutes had passed since the start of the attack, but the gardens and terrace were a scene of mass confusion and terror.

There was the sound of an animal yelping in pain overhead, and Victor looked up to see the Van Helsings' pet gargoyle flap away, the leathery membranes of its wings badly torn and its flanks deeply gashed.

"There he is!" a man's voice shouted. *"There's Todd!"*

A phalanx of vampire hunters outfitted in night-vision goggles and repeating crossbows were advancing up the stairs toward him. They were led by Christopher Van Helsing, head of the hated Institute and the direct descendant of those responsible for killing Victor's own parents.

"Open fire!"

It was too late to flee. Victor fell to the ground, his upper body so full of arrows it resembled a pincushion. Although none of the crossbow bolts had found his heart or pierced his skull, the only two vulnerable spots guaranteed to instantly kill a vampire, he was still too wounded to get back up onto his feet.

Christopher Van Helsing stepped forward, looking down at Victor with a bitter smile. "Every night since you killed my father, I've dreamed of this moment. Any last regrets, Todd?"

"Only that I didn't destroy you along with him," Victor growled, spitting a mouthful of blood onto his old enemy's shoes. "I guess this is what I get for being humane."

"At last, the Shadow Hand will finally be returned to its rightful heirs—and there is *nothing* you can do to stop it," Christopher Van Helsing sneered, planting his foot on the wounded vampire's chest. "This is for my dad," he said as he lifted his crossbow. "Burn in hell, Todd!"

"I'll be sure to give your father my regards when I arrive," Victor said with a humorless laugh.

"No!" Cally screamed as she lunged out of hiding, pushing the vampire hunter away from her father.

Christopher Van Helsing staggered backward, caught off guard, then quickly recovered, spinning around to find himself face-to-face with a girl with short-cropped dark hair and bright green eyes. Her left hand was glowing with a dark energy.

"Not you!" he gasped, a terrified look crossing his face.

Dropping his crossbow, Van Helsing cried out in pain and stared down at his forearm. On the sleeve of his jacket a black handprint could be seen. He stared in dumbstruck horror as the fingerprints began to elongate and spread like jungle vines, sending the blackness up his forearm and across his shoulder. As the unearthly darkness spread to his neck and face, Van Helsing screamed.

Cally covered her ears and looked away, unable to watch as the shadow poured itself into the vampire hunter's mouth and nose and eyes, filling him up from the outside in, like ink poured into a glass of water. Within seconds what had been a human being became a living silhouette. There were no eyes, no mouth, no features of any kind—just impenetrable blackness, as lightless as the depths of space. The living shadow waved its arms and staggered about for a moment, only to collapse on itself like the spray from a fountain.

Cally looked up and saw Peter standing on the other end of the terrace, staring at her in disbelief. The look of anger and loss in his eyes struck her heart like a hammer blow. Despite all her attempts to avoid it, the tradition of Todds and Van Helsings hating and killing one another had been passed along to a new generation.

There was a sound like the roar of a great dragon, and the remaining ballroom windows blew outward in a shower of flying glass as the imposing figure of Count Orlock emerged from the clouds of tear gas onto the terrace, gliding forward as if he were on casters. The Van Helsings, momentarily stunned by the demise of their leader, quickly snapped back to life, unleashing yet another volley at the approaching vampire lord.

Count Orlock did not flinch as the wall of arrows came whizzing toward him. He snatched one of the projectiles from midair as if it were nothing more than a toy. Snarling in disdain, he hurled it back at his enemies, skewering one of the vampire hunters through the throat. Van Helsing's troops began backing their way down the stairs, weapons still at the ready.

"By the Darkest Powers! You *dare* attack me in my own home?" Count Orlock shouted, his voice echoing like thunder from on high. "You *dare* to assault *my* people on *this*, one of our most cherished nights? You will pay for this affront with your wretched *lives*!" He raised his clawlike hands over his head, his eyes glowing bright red as lightning split the night sky. *"Arise, my legions!"* he bellowed. *"Arise and avenge your master!"*

In answer to his command, there was a deep rumbling noise. Massive subterranean gears began to turn as a half-dozen hidden entrances to the catacombs below King's Stone yawned open and the undead army of the Orlocks poured forth like angry ants. First out were the Roman centurions, dressed in their silvered armor and greaves, followed by gladiators outfitted with tridents and nets. Behind them came the medieval knights, sealed within their suits of plate armor, and grenadiers wearing Napoleonic uniforms.

Peter Van Helsing stared, dumbstruck, as the legions of undead swarmed in his direction. He barely responded as Rémy, one of his father's lieutenants, grabbed his arm.

"Peter—snap out of it! You've got to get out of here!"

"But—my dad . . ." Peter said thickly. The sight of his father being destroyed by the girl he loved had stunned him so profoundly it felt like his brain was drowning in molasses.

"Your father's gone! *You're* in charge now!" Rémy shouted as he dragged Peter toward the Stealth helicopters hidden at the far end of the garden. Van Helsings with flamethrowers strapped to their backs scurried forward, laying down a wall of fire between the advancing undead and their retreating comrades-in-arms.

Count Orlock's undead balked like skittish horses, unwilling to cross the burning line in pursuit of their prey. Although impervious to almost everything besides a stake to the heart and sunlight, the undead shared their masters' dread of fire.

As Rémy hurried him to the waiting choppers, Peter looked over his shoulder one last time and saw Cally standing on the terrace, staring after him with a stricken look on her face.

Peter cursed himself for being such a fool. He had allowed himself to fall under the spell of a vampire and it cost him his father's life. He had tried to tell himself that because Cally had a human mother, she wasn't like the others. There was no denying now that she was every bit her father's child. But that wasn't the worst of it.

No, the worst was that, even though he now hated her more than anything else on earth, he still craved her love. And always would.

"Cally! Praise to the Founders, you're alive! Are you okay?"

Cally stared mutely at Baron Metzger as he took off his jacket and draped it around her shoulders. She looked at her left arm. Although her hand was once more normal, she held it away from herself as if it was no longer a part of her body.

"I just wanted him to stop," she said numbly. "I didn't mean for it to happen. All I did was touch him. . . ."

"What are you talking about?" Baron Metzger frowned. "What's wrong?"

"She used the Shadow Hand to kill the leader of the Van Helsings," Victor grunted as he struggled to sit up. He grimaced as he pulled the arrows jutting from his torso free and tossed them aside.

"My liege—are you all right?" Metzger moved to his master's side, but Victor waved him away.

"I'll heal soon enough. I just need to find Lilith, that's all." Victor looked around the terrace, which was littered with the dead and dying from both sides. His eyes widened in alarm as he spotted the body of a blond woman sprawled near the stairs that led down to the garden. *"Merciful Founders—no!"* he cried out. *"Irina!"*

Victor dropped to his knees beside the body of his wife, a look of genuine shock on his face. "What was she doing out here? I told her to stay inside while I went to find Lilith!"

"Jules brought your wife and daughter to the safe room I have set aside for my family for such emergencies," Count Orlock explained. "Irina was trying to find you to let you know Lilith was safe." He shook his bald head in disgust. "This is my fault—I should have summoned my legions sooner!"

Metzger glanced down at his watch. "It's been less than eight minutes since the start of the attack," he said in amazement.

"Her heart is ruined," Victor said mournfully as he stroked his dead wife's hair. "Her bloodright is lost."

"The Van Helsings will pay for this transgression," Count Orlock assured him.

"They already have," Metzger replied. "Their leader is dead."

Count Orlock lifted an eyebrow. "Christopher Van Helsing is dead? How?"

Victor pointed at Cally, who stood shivering beside Metzger, clutching his jacket around her shoulders.

"You expect me to believe a mere *fledgling* brought down the leader of the Institute?" Orlock snorted.

"She is more than just a fledgling, Your Excellency," Victor explained. "The girl carries the Shadow Hand."

"Blood of the Founders!" Count Orlock turned to Metzger, a shocked look on his face. "Your daughter is half *human*?"

"Yes, Your Excellency."

"Once news of how Van Helsing died spreads among the other guests, there will have to be a board of inquiry," Orlock said, wearily massaging his furrowed brow. "De Laval will insist on it."

"I know, Boris," Metzger said grimly.

"Very well, Karl—take your child home before my brother-in-law finds out." Count Orlock sighed. "The slayer of our people's greatest enemy deserves that much, at least."

"When are we going to get out of here?" Lilith asked.

"When Uncle Boris comes to get us," Jules replied.

The Orlocks' secret panic room was a small chamber behind the huge fireplace that dominated the ballroom's west wall. Jules had spirited her to the hiding place after Lilith narrowly escaped the talons of the marauding gargoyle. Now she was sitting around with Jules, his father, Count de Laval, and his aunt Juliana, the Countess Orlock.

Lilith was relieved that Count Orlock was not hiding out with them, as being in such close quarters with someone that hideous was enough to make her gag. Still, she was worried that Xander hadn't shown up yet. He had been so brave—she hoped he hadn't gotten staked by a Van Helsing. Besides, she still needed his help in alchemy. Her mother had yet to return as well, but that was of considerably less concern to Lilith than getting off academic probation so she could go night-clubbing again—oh, yeah, and keep from flunking out of school.

There was the sound of stone scraping against stone as the concealed entrance swung open, revealing Count Orlock and Victor Todd in the doorway.

"Daddy!" Lilith squealed, throwing her arms around his neck.

"Are you okay, princess?" Victor asked, returning her hug.

"I got attacked by this gross-looking gargoyle! It would have killed me if not for Xander and his big brother, Klaus."

"Klaus is Xander's *demi*-brother," Count de Laval said, injecting himself into the conversation. "His mother was Count Orlock's first wife, *not* my sister."

"All that should matter to you, Julian, is that the boy saved your son's future bride," Count Orlock snapped.

Jules's father scowled at his kinsman's rebuke but said no more.

"Where's Irina?" Lilith asked, looking around. "She left to tell you I was safe. . . ."

"Lilith—I'm afraid I have some very bad news," Victor said solemnly. "Your mother is dead."

"Were you able to claim her bloodright before she died?" Lilith asked without missing a beat.

Victor shook his head. "No—there was no chance. Her heart was destroyed by a crossbow arrow."

Lilith shrieked. "Damn it! Damn-damn-damn-*damn!*" she wailed, kicking at the stone walls of the panic room in a blind rage.

Victor grabbed her by the wrists. "Calm down! I realize you're upset . . ."

"Why couldn't that stupid bitch just stay put?" Lilith spat, her blue eyes flashing in anger. "She didn't *have* to go looking for you! What was she thinking, putting my bloodright on the line like that? She had *no* right to go and get herself killed like that! No right at *all*!"

"Can't this car go any faster?" Cally asked anxiously. "I need to get home as soon as I can!"

Baron Metzger leaned over and patted her hand.

"You needn't worry, Cally. The Van Helsings have no leader. The son is little more than a pretty boy—he's dwelled in his father's shadow all his life. I doubt he'll be coming after us anytime soon, not after the losses they suffered tonight."

"I don't care about them coming after me. I'm worried about my *mother*."

"Why should Van Helsings bother with her? Besides, it's not like she's there by herself—your father left two of his undead in the apartment."

Cally looked out the window. "I just have a bad feeling, that's all."

"I have never been so embarrassed in my life—and that's saying something!" Victor snarled as he strode through the hallway of the Orlock mansion, Lilith trotting after him in her scuffed heels. "I realize you and your mother were never close—but you could at least *pretend* to be upset that she's dead!"

"But I *am* upset!" Lilith protested.

"No, you're *mad*! Mad at your *mother* for being killed! Believe it or not, there's a difference. You're not the only one inconvenienced by all this, you know. It bothers me that I've been cheated of Irina's bloodright, but at least I have the good sense not to publicly accuse her of getting killed on purpose!"

"I *never* said that!"

"Well, you're certainly *acting* like it! It wouldn't hurt for you to show your mother some respect."

"Yeah. Right." Lilith sneered. "That's a good one, coming from you."

Victor whipped around so fast she nearly collided with him. The look in her father's eyes as he glared at her made her cringe. "Don't you *ever* use that tone of voice with me again—understood?"

"Yes, sir," Lilith whispered, dropping her gaze.

"We must get away from here in case the human authorities show up," Victor said, resuming his hurried walk down the corridor. "Besides, I've got a *ton* of work ahead of me! When Irina died, all the Viesczy undead went with her, including a good number of the household staff. It's going to take time for me to bring enough of my family's undead out of cold storage to replace them. Plus there's the matter of your mother's totentanz: a woman of her stature and family line requires a magnificent celebration."

"Do we have enough undead?" Lilith asked anxiously.

"Don't worry—I have more than plenty. They've been warehoused for some time, so it might take them a little while to become acclimated to this century and its technology, but everything should be back to normal in a couple of weeks."

As they exited King's Stone, heading toward the

parking field, Lilith eyed the skies, half expecting to see a gargoyle swooping down at her. She shivered and hurried after her father. Victor paused for a second, searching the collection of luxury sedans and high-priced sports cars for his Rolls-Royce.

"I see it, Daddy!" Lilith said. "Third row to the left!" She frowned and looked around. "I don't see Vasily, though."

"He's right here," Victor replied, opening the car door to reveal an empty suit of clothes and a chauffeur's cap lying on the leather seat behind the steering wheel. On the floorboards sat a pair of black patent leather shoes, filled to overflowing with a fine, grayish-white powder. Victor leaned inside and swept the remains of the chauffeur out onto the gravel drive.

"I always thought Vasily belonged to the Todd side of the family." Lilith coughed, waving her hand in front of her face. "What are we going to do now?"

"I *do* know how to drive, you know," Victor replied sarcastically as he retrieved the keys to the car.

"The sooner we're away from here, the better!" Lilith said as she opened the rear door.

"Where do you think you're going?" her father growled. "You're sitting up front with me."

"But—"

"No buts, young lady! I'm not going to have people think I'm your damned chauffeur. Now get in the car."

"All right! I *hear* you!" Lilith exclaimed, slamming the rear door shut.

Victor shook his head in dismay as he slid the Rolls into gear. He was already starting to miss Irina. And whether she wanted to admit it or not, so was Lilith.

CHAPTER 4

The first thing Cally noticed as she stepped out of the elevator was the silence. She glanced up at Baron Metzger. "I don't like it. It's too quiet. Usually you can hear whatever movie my mom is watching the moment the doors open."

"Perhaps her home theater system has been dismantled?"

"I guess," Cally conceded. Maybe there was a simple, innocent answer after all. Maybe the Baron was right: she was simply being paranoid and her mother was okay. The last time she was in the apartment Walther and Sinclair, the two undead servants her father had assigned to her relocation, were busily packing up the Montures' belongings so they could be shipped overseas. However, as Cally walked down the hall toward her apartment, she saw that the door was hanging crookedly on busted hinges, its dead bolt shattered.

After months of enduring her mother's wall-shaking home theater system, the neighbors had no doubt learned to tune out loud noises coming from their apartment. They probably wrote off sounds from the break-in as simply sound effects from yet another movie.

"Mom!" Cally cried. She lunged for the broken door, but Baron Metzger stopped her.

"You stay here," he said firmly. "I'll go in. Your father will have my head on a platter—and I don't mean figuratively—if anything happens to you."

Cally wanted to argue, but the look Metzger gave her made it clear he was not going to tolerate any dissent. She grudgingly nodded and stepped aside, watching as he entered through the ruined door. A few moments later he reemerged from the apartment with a grim look on his face.

"What's going on? What happened?" Cally asked, bobbing up and down, trying to peer over his shoulders. "Where's my mother? Is she hurt? *Mom?* Mom, it's me!" she shouted as she tried to push past the Baron.

"You don't want to go in there, Cally." Metzger shook his head. "There are three bodies: two male and one female."

"What?" Cally gasped. "I don't believe you! I want to see for myself!"

Metzger held her arms, pinning them to her sides. "Take it from me; you *do not* want to see your mother like that! The Van Helsings must have thought she was one of us. . . ."

"No—you're wrong. I *know* you are!" Cally kept shaking her head, as if by denying what she was being told she could somehow change reality. "You *have* to be!"

"She was holding this," Metzger said. He reached into his coat pocket and gave her a small framed photograph. Cally stared at the snapshot of her grandparents, taken on their final wedding anniversary together, until the tears made it impossible to see.

Her mother had wanted nothing more than to be part of vampire society. She had completely immersed herself in their culture from adolescence onward. Although Sheila Monture could never truly "live" as a vampire, her daughter took a weird comfort in knowing she had died like one.

As she wiped the tears from her face with the back of her hand, it occurred to Cally that all her human relatives were dead. The realization was both sobering and frightening. "What am I going to do now?" she wondered aloud.

"Well, you certainly can't remain here," Baron Metzger replied. "It's too dangerous."

"But—I have nowhere else to go."

Metzger placed a protective arm around her

shoulders. "How would you like to come live with me for a while?" he asked gently.

"What about my clothes? All I have to wear is what's on my back. Everything else is packed."

"Let me worry about that," he said soothingly. "I'll arrange for your things to be brought over."

"Are you sure this is okay?" she asked uncertainly. "I don't want to be any bother. . . ."

"Don't be silly, my dear! You're no trouble at all!" Baron Metzger assured her. "It's not much—just an apartment I keep for my trips to New York. But you should be comfortable enough for the time being. You'll even have your own room."

Cally felt like a swimmer who had been caught up by a huge wave and thrown on the beach. For the last two years, ever since her grandmother's death, she had worked tirelessly to take care of and provide for her mother. Although she was ashamed to admit it, part of her was relieved to be able to simply be a child again and allow herself to be taken care of.

"To the Plaza," Baron Metzger told his chauffeur as he helped his foster daughter into the car. "And step on it."

Straddling Fifty-eighth and Fifty-ninth streets along Fifth Avenue, the Plaza had been host to the glamor-ously wealthy for over a century. Although it had begun its life as a traditional hotel, as part of its multi-million-dollar restoration it now offered permanent private residences for those who could afford the price.

Cally stared in mute amazement at the polished marble floors, gleaming chandeliers, and decorated ceilings as they walked across the lobby to the building's famous gilded elevators. As a child she had eagerly devoured the Eloise books and often daydreamed about living in a fancy hotel just like she did. If not for the tragic circumstances surrounding her relocation, Cally would have been elated to get the chance to walk in the fictional footsteps of her childhood hero.

On their arrival at Metzger's fourteenth-floor apartment, the front door was opened by an undead servant dressed in formal butler's livery, complete with white gloves.

"Welcome home, Baron," the servant said as he relieved his master of his coat.

"Thank you, Edgar," Metzger replied. "Prepare the guest room for the young lady."

"As you wish, sir," Edgar replied.

"It's not very big," Metzger said, gesturing to the seven-room apartment with its high ceilings, ornate moldings, and period mantelpieces, "but it's cozy."

"It certainly is," Cally replied, eyeing the signature Versace home decor.

"Please forgive me for a few moments, my dear," the

Baron said. "I need to make some phone calls."

Cally walked across the parquet floor to the living room window that faced Fifth Avenue. From where she stood, Central Park looked like a giant blanket unfurled at her feet, embroidered with winding strings of lights that were the old-style lampposts that lined its paths and byways. Everything had happened so fast, she had yet to truly take it all in. Things in her life were changing forever, with no time for good-byes. It was almost as if everything tonight had happened to someone else.

As she stared out at the park, she wondered if her father was still planning to send her away to Europe. The thought of going to a strange country without her mother kindled a flicker of anxiety that quickly grew, burning its way through the protective layer of numbness. She had always had family around her. But her grandmother was long gone, and her mother . . . her mother was . . . She could not bring herself to finish the thought, at least not yet.

She let out a shuddering breath as she glanced down at the windowsill and saw a drop of water strike its edge. She reached up and touched her face to discover she was crying.

"I have good news," Metzger said as he reentered the room. "I spoke to your father, and he's decided it's no longer necessary for you to leave New York." He froze as he saw her rub the tears from her cheeks. "Are you still weeping?" he asked, a hint of surprise in his voice.

"I always knew I would outlive my mother," Cally said, fighting to control the quaver in her voice. "I just never thought it would be like this."

"Although I am not your father, perhaps I can pass along a little paternal advice," the Baron said gently as he steered her over to the sofa. "I realize that you are not completely like us and that you were raised with human mores and morals, so please, do not take what I am about to say the wrong way: if you are to live among us, you cannot mourn your mother beyond this night."

"What?" Cally blinked in disbelief.

"It is not the way of our people to grieve our dead as humans do," Metzger explained. "We celebrate them with a great party in their honor, and once that is over, we simply go on with our lives as we did before."

"Are you telling me I have to *forget* my mother?" Cally asked. Although aghast by what Metzger was saying, she felt compelled to listen.

"The average human lives, what? Seventy-five? Eighty-five years, at best? Our span numbers in the centuries. To spend hundreds of years mourning the loss of a loved one—the pain as fresh a decade from now as it is today—is a torment you never want to endure. Grieving in public is forbidden in our world, for fear it will spread melancholy to those around you."

"Does that mean I can go back home?" Cally asked hopefully as she wiped the tears from her cheeks.

Baron Metzger shook his head. "As I said earlier, it's far too dangerous for you to be on your own, especially now that the Van Helsings know where to find you. You'll live with me. You *are* supposed to be my daughter, after all."

"But why bother with the charade?" Cally frowned. "Irina is dead. What difference does it make now?"

"Because your father doesn't want to alienate his future in-laws," Metzger explained. "He's worked hard to arrange a marriage with the de Lavals. Julian is a Purist, just like the delightful Mr. Mauvais you met earlier. If he knew Lilith had a half-human sister, he'd call the whole thing off."

"The guest room is ready, master," Edgar said. "I've taken the liberty of drawing the young lady a bath."

"Very good!" Baron Metzger said. "You've had a rough night—perhaps you would like some time to yourself?"

"Thank you, Baron," Cally said wearily. "You're right, I *am* tired."

"I'll bid you good morning, then." Metzger smiled, patting her hand. "And remember, my dear: life is too long for sorrow."

* * *

The guest room was not only twice the size of her bedroom in Williamsburg, it also had its own bathroom. Like the rest of the apartment, it was furnished in Versace, which, despite her earlier comment to Baron Metzger, came across as more sterile than cozy. As she looked around her new surroundings, Cally found herself missing her funky canopy bed, her old wardrobe, and the patchwork mural of posters that covered the back of her bedroom door.

As she slipped out of her clothes, she glanced at the medicine cabinet over the sink and saw that the mirror had been painted over with flat eggshell matte. It was a jarring reminder that from here on in, she would be living completely in the vampire world. Up until now, even though she had extensive dealings with vampire society, both Old Blood and New, her home life had been human.

Cally carefully folded her evening gown and placed it on the small dressing bench next to the door before stepping into the waiting bath, the surface of which was covered with scattered rose petals. She normally preferred taking showers, but sometimes she needed to unwind with a good long soak.

She picked up the bath sponge and squeezed it onto her shoulders and breasts. As she closed her eyes, her mother's face flashed before her. Suddenly the numbness that filled her began to crack, like ice in a spring thaw. She gasped aloud as the pain pushed its way into her, filling her heart like floodwaters breaching a dam.

Ever since she was a baby, Cally had enjoyed the supernatural stamina and vitality of her vampire heritage. She had never been ill a day in her life, and what physical pain she was forced to endure had always been brief. She had never truly known suffering, as most humans understand the word. At least not physically, anyway. The emotional kind she knew all too well.

The last time she'd experienced such anguish was when Granny died, two years ago. The suffering she had endured was so overwhelming and lasted for so long, it frightened her like nothing else in her life had before. And now here she was, feeling it yet again, only now it seemed a thousand times worse.

At least with her grandmother's death there had been time to prepare for the inevitable, and there was some comfort in knowing Granny was no longer in pain. But her mother's death had been so sudden and cruel and . . . her fault. Cally wrapped her arms around her knees, rocking back and forth in the rose-strewn bathwater as she surrendered to her grief.

I should have been there. I should have protected her. It was me *they were looking for, not her. Mom, the attack, Peter's father, Lilith's mother . . . It's all* my *fault.*

CHAPTER 5

Cally sees herself walking barefoot across the beach, watching the tide come in. She is wearing a color-ful sarong, a hibiscus tucked behind one ear. The light from the full moon makes the gently lapping waves breaking against the shore look black and silver. Towering palm trees sway their heads in the balmy breeze, marking the start of the jungle that covers the rest of the island.

She looks down and spots a conch shell washed up onto the shore. Smiling, she plucks her prize from the foam and puts its pink curving rim to her ear. Instead of hearing the ocean, however, she hears someone call-ing to her as if from a great distance. Cally frowns and lets the conch drop back onto the sand.

She looks up the beach and sees a male figure

standing atop a dune, silhouetted against the night sky. As she watches, he motions for her to join him. Although she cannot make out his features, she somehow knows that he is Peter. She waves to him as she runs across the wet sand, hurrying to catch up.

As Cally draws closer to Peter, she hears someone calling her name again, only this time it is coming from the ocean. She turns to look and is alarmed to see her mother floundering in the surf, fifty feet from shore. She starts toward the water, only to be brought up short when Peter grabs her.

Cally looks at Peter, trying to figure out why he wants to stop her from rescuing her mother, only to realize that the person holding her back isn't him at all. Standing in his place is a thing made of living shadow, with swirling knots of nothing where a face should be. Although it has no eyes, somehow she knows it can see her.

Cally watches helplessly as the current takes her frantically struggling mother somewhere she can never follow. She tries to wrench herself free of the shadow thing's grip but is unable to break its hold. She looks down at her wrist and is startled to see rivulets of darkness twining their way up her arm, like vines climbing a trellis.

Cally, where are you? her mother calls out forlornly. *Why aren't you here?*

* * *

Cally woke up gasping, tangled in her bedclothes, her body slick with sweat. Her heart was pounding in her chest as if she'd just run a marathon. She didn't recognize her surroundings at first and looked around in vain for the familiar touchstones of her old bedroom: the armoire, her sewing machine, and the tailor's dummy.

As she struggled to banish the fear that had followed her into the waking world, she wasn't sure if she was still dreaming or not. Her left arm felt ice-cold and fire-hot at the same time. Looking down, she could see that her forearm was covered in shadow, as if she had dipped it up to the elbow in a bucket of tar.

Fighting back the urge to panic, she remembered what her grandmother, Sina, had said about controlling her stormgathering powers: *Ride* with *the power; don't let the power ride* you.

Cally took a deep breath, letting it out slowly as she deliberately lowered her heartbeat. All she needed to do was calm down. When she reopened her eyes, she was relieved to see that the darkness had drained away, returning to wherever it had come from.

She lifted her hand, wiggling her fingers as she studied them for any trace of lingering shadow.

In the names of the Founders, what am I turning into?

* * *

Lilith frowned at the digital clock next to her bed. Where in sweet hell was Esmeralda? Lilith had been waiting almost twenty minutes for her dresser, which was virtually unheard of. Esmeralda *knew* she couldn't start her evening without having her makeup and hair done.

The little gypsy tart better have a good excuse for keeping her waiting. Strike that: there was no such thing as an excuse when it came to the undead. It's not like they had busy social calendars to keep track of or family emergencies.

Things would be so much easier if she could simply apply her own makeup and style her own hair. But since mirrors were forbidden in vampire homes, she had no choice but to rely on her dresser to make her look presentable. Assuming she ever showed up.

Lilith picked up the telephone on her bedside table and punched the in-house line. A second later the Todds' head butler answered.

"Yes, Miss Lilith?"

"Curtis, I've been waiting *forever* for Esmeralda to dress me! Where is she?"

"I'm sorry, Miss Lilith," Curtis replied in his cultured British voice. "Esmeralda is no longer with us."

Lilith frowned. "Huh? Where did she go?"

"Esmeralda was one of Madame Irina's undead," the

⚜ 59 ⚜

butler explained. "She no longer exists, I'm afraid."

Lilith scowled. "Then get me another dresser—immediately!"

"One has already been withdrawn from cold storage, Miss Lilith. She should be on the way up as we speak."

Just then there was a knock at her door. Lilith opened the bedroom door and found herself looking at a woman wearing a low-waisted slip dress and a cloche hat, carrying the telltale makeup valise of a dresser.

"Hello. My name is Josette." The new servant squinted at Lilith, a confused look on her face. "Is that *you*, Madame Irina?"

"No!" Lilith said sharply. "Madame Irina is no more. I'm her daughter."

"Daughter?" Josette's plucked eyebrows climbed in surprise. "Then the master finally succeeded in producing an heir?"

"Well, *duh*," Lilith said, rolling her eyes as she headed back into the bathroom. "Let's get on with it—I've got places to be, and I've been kept waiting long enough as it is."

"As you wish, mistress." Josette bowed her head.

Lilith turned and stared at her dresser with a startled look on her face. "*What* did you just call me?"

"I called you 'mistress,' that is all," Josette replied.

"You said Madame Irina is dead. That makes you the mistress of the Todd family, does it not?"

"Yeah, I guess it does," Lilith said thoughtfully. "It's just that I never really thought of it in those terms before now."

As Lilith sat down in her makeup chair, Josette took out a black silk barber's drape and gave it a brisk snap before fixing it around her mistress's neck.

"So—what movie star do you want to look like? Theda Bara? Gloria Swanson? Ooh! I know! How about Lillian Gish?"

Lilith found her father seated at the head of the dining room table with his BlackBerry pressed to his ear and a disconcerted look on his face.

"This is *very* short notice! You know what my situation is. Are you certain something like this is really *necessary*? Yes, yes, I realize the potential danger—it's just that I don't see *how* you can compare this situation to what happened before." Victor closed his eyes and heaved a sigh of resignation. "Very well. I'll be there as soon as I can."

"Who was that?" Lilith asked as she poured herself a goblet of AB neg from the plasma warmer mounted atop the buffet.

"Just someone at HemoGlobe," Victor replied, quickly sliding the BlackBerry into the breast pocket of his jacket. "We have to restructure in order to cover the unexpected losses to the workforce. Your mother controlled many of them."

"You're not going to go out of business because of this, are you?" Lilith asked anxiously.

"Don't be silly," Victor replied. "As I told you last night, I still have plenty of undead in cold storage, spread throughout this country and Europe, to make up the difference. But I won't lie to you—the transition phase is bound to be a bit bumpy. The older undead have to get up to speed on the current technology and culture."

"I know what you mean," Lilith said as she finished the last of her blood. "It took me nearly a half hour to talk the dresser Curtis picked to replace Esmeralda from tricking me out like some old movie star. I gave her a stack of fashion magazines to study before tomorrow night." Having finished her waking meal, she turned to address the butler. "Curtis, ring up Bruno and have him bring my car around."

"Yes, mistress," Curtis replied automatically, bowing at the waist.

"Not so fast," Victor said, staying Curtis with a motion of his hand. He fixed his daughter with a baffled frown. "Where do you think *you're* going?"

"To the club," Lilith replied as she casually reached for her coat.

"You're not doing anything of the sort!" Victor barked. "Just because your mother was slain last night doesn't mean I've changed my mind! Until you pass your Basic Alchemy class, the only places you're allowed to go outside of school are the Central Scrivenery and your tutor's laboratory."

"You're not being fair!" Lilith protested, angrily hurling her Nanette Lepore coat onto the floor.

"I'm not in the mood tonight, Lilith!" Victor warned her. "It's bad enough I have to spread myself thin trying to keep HemoGlobe afloat while arranging for your mother's totentanz. The last thing I need from you right now is *attitude*!"

Lilith glowered at her father, her hands balled into fists. Although she and Irina had never been close, at that moment she wished her mother were still alive so she could run and tell her everything about Victor and his little half-human bastard just to spite him.

But Irina was dead and Lilith's trump card was now worthless. It seemed she couldn't win for losing—but that didn't stop a girl from having plans.

From the outside, Xander's laboratory looked like any of the other aging office buildings that lined the streets of the Flatiron District.

"I'll call you when I'm ready to go home, Bruno," Lilith said as she stepped out onto the curb.

The lobby of the building was outfitted in marble and brass furnishings dating back to World War I. Hanging next to the elevator, locked inside a case of glass, was an alphabetical listing of the various businesses in the building. XOXperiments was on the top floor.

Lilith stepped inside the aged elevator car and punched the button for the sixth floor. When the doors opened, Xander Orlock was there to greet her.

"Wow, this is really some place you've got here, Exo," she said. Several workbenches were placed throughout the large, open room, each set up with a different collection of alchemic instruments. An apothecary's crocodile, such as those used in ancient Egyptian rituals, was suspended by wires from the pressed tin ceiling.

"My dad gave me this place after I accidentally blew a hole in my bedroom wall," Xander said sheepishly. "It used to be a photography studio, so the neighbors are used to weird chemical smells. I also have private access to the roof, so I can come and go whenever I like."

Lilith raised an eyebrow in surprise. "You fly a lot?"

Xander nodded. "I'm the sub-captain of my Aerial Combat team."

"I should have known from the way you tackled that gargoyle!" she said, nodding appreciatively. "Thank you for saving me last night, by the way."

"I didn't really do that much—it was mostly Kayo."

"Kayo?"

"That's my nickname for my big brother, Klaus. He's the one who attacked the gargoyle. I just happened to be there to catch you."

"Yeah, but you went after that thing, too. That was pretty brave of you."

"Well, I couldn't let my brother tackle it by himself, could I?" A look of embarrassment abruptly crossed Xander's face, as if he'd suddenly remembered something important. "Oh, yeah—I heard about your mom. Sorry."

"Yeah, well. Things happen," Lilith said with a shrug as she walked over to one of the workbenches. "Like your cousin cheating on me."

"I don't understand *why* Jules does things like that," Xander said in exasperation. "You are *so* much prettier than Carmen!"

"You really think so?" Lilith placed her hands over her face, tracing the geometry of her features with her fingertips. "Everyone *tells* me I'm beautiful, but how can I know that for sure? I mean, people say things they don't mean all the time."

"Well, I meant *every* word," Xander assured her.

At first Lilith thought he was being sarcastic, but when she looked into his clear blue eyes, she could tell he was sincere. "Thanks, Exo," she said, blushing slightly. "That's good to hear." She paused for a second, thoughtfully tapping her chin. "Do you remember me asking you about whether or not it might be possible to create a means of allowing our kind to cast a reflection?"

"Of course." He nodded. "It's an intriguing proposition."

"I'm glad you said that," she said with a smile. "Tell me, Exo—what do you know about cosmetics?"

Cally wandered through Baron Metzger's apartment, taking in the twenty-four-carat-gold bathroom faucets, the marble backsplashes in the kitchen, and the crystal chandeliers. She had been so overwhelmed when she first arrived that she had not really had a chance to fully appreciate the perks that came with living in the Plaza. Too bad Sheila wasn't there to see it.

Cally closed her eyes and shook her head as the thought crossed her mind. The hurt was too new, too raw for her to tolerate for more than a few seconds. To dwell on it would only lead to tears—and that was the last thing she needed if she was going to survive in her new world.

As she wandered down the hallways back toward her bedroom, Cally noticed that the door to Baron Metzger's office was standing ajar. Curious, she poked her head inside—just to check it out, she told herself.

The office resembled the den of a Victorian gentlemen's club, with plenty of old leather and heavy wood furniture. An antique desk sat facing the door, its roll top raised to reveal a flat-screen computer monitor. The walls of the room were lined with barrister bookcases filled with canisters containing scrolls and manuscripts in chthonic script, the written language of the vampire race.

Hanging over the desk was an oil portrait of a man who bore a strong family resemblance to Baron Metzger, dressed in the style of the early seventeenth century, the lace cravat done to perfection. It was the kind of painting you'd expect to find hanging in a museum, not in someone's house.

Cally walked over to the desk and picked up a stack of paper next to the computer. As she fanned through it, she realized the sheets were photocopies of sketches for the new Maison d'Ombres ready-to-wear collection.

Although the basic designs were solid, they looked far too matronly for Cally's taste. She plucked a piece of parchment from one of the pigeonholes lining the upper portion of the desk and, using a scrivening talon lying on the desk, began to sketch out her own version of the same outfits.

"What are you doing in my office?"

Cally was so startled by the sound of Baron Metzger's

voice that she jumped. Lost in what she was doing, she'd forgotten where she was. She turned to find her host looming over her, a perturbed look on his face.

"Oh! I'm sorry, Baron! I was just looking around and I saw these sketches. . . . I was bored, and I started doodling. . . ."

"May I see them?" Metzger asked, holding out his hand.

Cally meekly handed the parchment over. "I'm really sorry if I overstepped my bounds. I realize I'm a guest in your house. . . ."

The Baron's eyebrows rose so high they disappeared into his hairline. "Don't be sorry, my dear," he said as he studied Cally's sketches. "The changes you've made to these designs really are quite clever."

"I beg your pardon, Baron," the butler said as he stepped into the room.

"Yes, Edgar?" Metzger said. "What is it?"

"There is a Mr. Mauvais here to see you. He says he is on Synod business."

"I'll be there directly, Edgar." Metzger set aside the sketches and motioned for Cally to follow him.

Anton Mauvais stood in the living room, scowling up at the Picasso hanging over the mantelpiece. Around his neck hung the seal of a Synod: an amulet resembling a clock face.

"Good evening, Anton," Metzger said as he entered

the room. "To what do I owe the pleasure of this visit?"

"There is a board of inquiry being held this evening to address the question of your daughter," Mauvais said sourly. "You are both to come with me to the Naos."

CHAPTER 6

Cally anxiously looked around as she and Baron Metzger were led across the Central Park West office building's polished marble lobby. The elevator took them to the lowest level, buried deep beneath the streets of the city. On exiting, they were met by a pair of well-muscled undead with submachine guns slung over their shoulders. The red epaulets on their leather trench coats marked them as Crimson Guards, the private army of the Lord Chamberlain.

Cally and the Baron were led down a long, low brick-lined tunnel to an iron door inscribed with a larger version of the amulet Mauvais wore around his neck. Mounted in its center was the chthonic ideogram for the word *blood* cast in gold. The door opened with a squealing sound. Standing on the threshold was an older man with a long beard and robust build, dressed in the scarlet robes of an archpriest.

"Greetings, Father Lazarus," Mauvais said. "Have the others arrived?"

"They are all here," the archpriest replied, stepping away to allow the newcomers entrance.

They walked into a huge, circular room with a forty-foot vaulted ceiling. This was the Naos, the shrine dedicated to the thirteen Founders of the vampire race. Twelve alcoves were set into the walls. In each one stood a twenty-foot-tall idol fashioned from ebony. In the very center of the chamber, positioned like the angle on a sundial, stood the idol dedicated to the thirteenth and most powerful of the Founders: Urlok the Terrible, whose winged arms were held open as if in welcome. Or attack.

Count Orlock and Victor Todd, along with a man Cally did not recognize, were seated at a large stone table positioned in front of Urlok. At either end of the table were more Crimson Guards, who stared at her like automatons.

"Come forward, Metzger—it is time for you to answer for your sins against the Blood," the third man said grimly.

"Whether Baron Metzger has sinned against the Blood has yet to be determined, Count de Laval," Count Orlock interjected. "That is what this board of inquiry is to decide."

"Count de Laval? Are you Jules's father?" Cally asked. "He was my escort at the Grand Ball. . . ."

"Don't remind me," he sniffed.

"Frankly, I don't understand why you're insisting on this inquiry, Julian," Victor said testily. "You should be *praising* this girl as a hero, not condemning her as a threat! She not only saved my life, she single-handedly destroyed the greatest enemy of her people!"

"'Her people'? Ha!" Count de Laval sneered. "She's *not* a vampire, Victor!"

"Yet neither is she human," Count Orlock pointed out. "However, these arguments do not address the central issue before this board. Baron Metzger, why did you represent your hybrid daughter as being a true-blood at the Rauhnacht Grand Ball?"

"I admit my deceit, but my decision was made out of pride, not malice," Metzger replied. "Throughout her life, I have been forced to deny Cally as my child for fear of how my wife might react. Once I became a widower, I was finally free to claim my daughter. She is a magnificent girl—incredibly smart and talented. Did you know she started developing stormgathering talents before the age of twelve?"

Count Orlock lifted an eyebrow, apparently impressed. "Really? That young?"

"I don't care if she can juggle chain saws while reciting Proust!" Count de Laval snarled. "You have made a deliberate mockery of one of our most cherished traditions!"

Baron Metzger squared his shoulders, refusing to be intimidated. "I realize that Purists such as yourself see no value in human blood beyond slaking your thirst, but *all* vampires have some human DNA in them, no matter how little: even *you*, Count de Laval!

"Whether we like it or not, humans aren't the frightened cavemen our ancestors preyed on anymore. The only hope for the vampire race's continued existence is *more* interbreeding with humans, not *less*! We're being strangled in an ever-tightening noose of technology—cameras are everywhere! Pretty soon we'll be pushed back to the caves. The Institute will be the least of our worries then."

Count de Laval leaped to his feet, striking the table-top hard with his fist. *"Heresy!"*

"Were the Founders heretics, then?" Victor replied. "Baron Metzger is right: we wouldn't exist if vampires hadn't bred with humans in the past. There is *nothing* in the scrolls forbidding the Grand Ball to those with human blood in their veins. It merely states that any female child being presented must have at least *one* parent of the Old Blood. Cally meets that requirement."

"I should have known you would take up for Metzger!" Count de Laval spat in disgust. "You're his liege lord!"

"Victor is correct," Count Orlock said. "There is nothing that specifically prohibits hybrids from participating in the Grand Ball. Why, I recall back in 1703 when a kinsman of my first wife introduced his half-human daughter, Grozda, at the Grand Ball in Kiev—"

"Be that as it may," Count de Laval growled, cutting off Count Orlock in mid-anecdote, "we all know what happened the *last* time the Shadow Hand was made manifest! I say it's better to get rid of her now than run the risk of her going rogue!"

Victor Todd stood to make his point. "Despite what you believe, Count de Laval, Cally is *not* Pieter Van Helsing. She has not suffered the same cruelty Pieter did at the hands of his father's people. She doesn't hate us—at least not yet. With her we have an opportunity that we squandered with Pieter—a second chance to take the Shadow Hand's power and make it work *for* us instead of *against* us. Then we would never have to live in fear of human attack ever again!"

"I'll admit some of what you say intrigues me, Victor," Count de Laval said grudgingly. "But I still say the risk is too great to allow the child to live. What is your opinion, Boris?"

"My family has learned the folly of valuing the purity of our bloodright above all things," Count Orlock said solemnly. "Baron Metzger is right: there is no returning to the old days. To continue to fold inward does nothing but diminish us." He rose from his chair and lifted his eyes to the vaulted ceiling. "Come forward, Klaus. It's all right, son—you can show yourself now."

Cally followed the Count's gaze and saw what looked like a storybook demon roosting on the shoulder of one of the idols, staring down at her with black eyes the size of saucers. She instinctively gasped as the creature unfurled the pinioned, batlike wings on its back and swooped down from its perch.

The eldest son of Count Orlock was close to seven feet tall and covered in smooth, close-cropped gray fur, with knees that hinged backward. Unlike the winged form taken by normal vampires, Klaus had a pair of wings growing out of his back, set above a pair of perfectly normal, fully functional human arms.

"By the Darkest Powers! You brought that monstrosity *here*?" Count de Laval hissed indignantly.

"You can't have it both ways, Julian," Count Orlock told his brother-in-law. "You can't condemn the 'dilution' of the vampire race while at the same time reviling the result of inbreeding." He held out his hand to Klaus, who scurried to his father's side. Count Orlock smiled fondly as he scratched his eldest child behind the ears. "When he was born, I was told I should destroy him, just as he destroyed my beloved wife. They called him a freak, a throwback—everything but what he is: my son.

"I know what it is like to be proud of a child others

revile, to desire the best for him, even when you know it is impossible," Count Orlock said, smiling at Baron Metzger. "Because of that, I cannot find it in my heart to condemn you for what you have done. In fact, if your daughter had not been at the Grand Ball the other night, I daresay the outcome would have been far worse than it was. I, too, believe that we have been given a unique opportunity here, one that we dare not squander out of fear. As ranking Synodist for the City of New York, I propose that Cally Monture be released to the custody of her father, Baron Karl Metzger, and that she be subject to regular monitoring and inspection by Synod officials to determine whether or not she is a genuine threat to the vampire race."

"Thank you, Your Excellency," Baron Metzger said, bowing his head in gratitude.

"This is *outrageous*!" Count de Laval sputtered. "I can't believe what I'm hearing! I'm going to appeal this decision to the Lord Chamberlain himself!"

"Just go ahead and do that," Count Orlock replied icily.

Count de Laval gathered himself up and marched out of the Naos. As Anton Mauvais turned to follow his liege, he fixed the Baron with an angry glare.

"I wouldn't get too attached to the brat if I were you, Metzger," he whispered. "This is far from over."

CHAPTER 7

"That's okay, Edgar!" Cally shouted over her shoulder as she hurried past the butler to answer the buzzer. Having been raised without servants, undead or otherwise, she was far more comfortable doing things herself. "I'll get it!"

Edgar stopped in his tracks. "Yes, Miss Cally," he replied before returning to wherever it was he lurked in between household tasks.

"Thanks for coming by." Cally smiled as she opened the door.

"No problem," Melinda Mauvais said, looking around as she entered apartment. "Wow! Nice place! But don't you live in Williamsburg?"

"Not anymore," Cally replied vaguely, unwilling to go into any further detail for fear of stirring up emotions best left unseen. "This is where I'm staying now."

"My father said something about you being brought before the Synod. Is that true?"

"Sorta." Cally shrugged. "But everything worked out okay. Although I don't think your dad likes me very much."

"My dad's an asshole," Melinda replied as she flopped down on the living room sofa. "After we got home from the Grand Ball, he gave me this lecture about how he doesn't want me hanging out with you anymore because you're half human."

"Aren't you afraid of him getting mad when he finds out you're still friends with me?" Cally asked.

"I think my *own* thoughts and live my *own* life, thank you very much. But you know that already— you've met my friend from Chinatown, remember? Besides, are *you* worried about your father's liege lord finding out about the Maledetto sisters?"

"I see your point," Cally said with a smile.

"So, what do you want to do tonight?" Melinda asked. "We could go check out this club I heard about."

"I don't feel like clubbing. . . . I was thinking we could go to Sister Midnight's."

"I *love* shopping there!" Melinda exclaimed, her face brightening. "She *always* stocks the cutest shoes! Are you looking for a new outfit?"

"Not exactly," Cally replied. "I want to talk to her

about carrying a line of clothes I've designed."

"Girl, you're kidding me—right?" Melinda said excitedly.

"No, I'm being totally straight." Cally laughed, holding up Sister Midnight's business card. "She *really* liked the evening gown I designed for the Grand Ball. See? She gave me this."

"Let me see!" Melinda squealed, snatching the embossed card out of her friend's hand. "*Ooohhh!* This is so great! I can't believe it!"

"I just need to get a couple of samples to take with me," Cally explained.

"Hurry up and pick something, then!" Melinda said, shooing her friend out of the room.

Unlike stores owned and operated by humans, which had bright lighting designed to show the merchandise off to its best advantage, the interior of Sister Midnight's resembled a romantically lit restaurant. After all, the select clientele who browsed the aisles all had excellent night vision.

Cally looked admiringly at the glossy black cabinetry and smoked glass counters of the sales floor, trying to picture one of her creations on the chic mannequin posed before the cosmetics counter.

An undead salesclerk, her hair pulled up into a fashionably severe bun, stepped forward.

"Welcome to Sister Midnight's." Her gaze dropped down to the garment bag draped over Cally's arm. "Do you have a return?"

"No, I'm here to see the owner. She gave me this." Cally handed the salesclerk the business card she'd shown Melinda.

"Wait right here. I'll fetch the mistress."

"There's no need—I'm already here," Sister Midnight said, stepping out from behind a rack of cashmere dresses. "Cally, my dear!" she exclaimed, opening her arms in welcome. "I heard how you saved Victor Todd from that wretched Christopher Van Helsing! Your father must be *so* proud of you right now! It is an *honor* to have you in my shop!"

"Yes, well, I remembered what you said about liking my dress," Cally replied, blushing at the older woman's praise.

"Are these some more of your creations?" Sister Midnight asked, taking the garment bag out of Cally's hands. "I trust you brought me something *fabulous*! Come—let's go to my office, shall we?"

"Can my friend join us?" Cally asked, taking Melinda's hand in her own.

"If it makes you happy, I don't see why not."

Sister Midnight quickly ushered the girls into a room at the back of the store. She placed the garment bag on her desk and unzipped it. While she inspected the clothes, Cally and Melinda stared in awe at the wall of autographed photographs of famed designers and fashion models, all of them signed to *Sis*.

"Did you really meet Coco Chanel?" Cally asked.

"*Meet* her?" Sister Midnight laughed. "Darling, where do you think she got the idea for that little black dress? As for you, young lady, I really like the iridescent midnight blue wrap dress you have here—especially the way it puffs out below the waist. And this appliquéd denim skirt is absolutely *precious*! Did you do all this needlework by hand? *Most* impressive!

"I've been steadily losing younger customers over the last few years to the human boutiques and brands, and I think this might be just what I need to bring them back into the shop. Would you be interested in presenting your collection here at the boutique?"

"You mean a fashion show?" Cally gasped. "A *real* fashion show?"

"You'll need at *least* twelve looks," Sister Midnight warned her. "Is that a problem?"

"Not at all!" Cally replied, even though she knew she had nowhere near that many pieces ready to go.

"Very good. I'll keep these two outfits and have my seamstresses fit them to the runway models we'll be using for the show. That'll leave you with ten more." She pulled a BlackBerry out of her jacket pocket. "How does two weeks from now sound?"

"Great!" Cally smiled, trying not to panic.

"This is going to be *the* event of the season, my dear!" Sister Midnight enthused. "I mean, you've already got serious buzz working for you! Slaying the head of the Van Helsing Institute? Sweetheart, you couldn't buy that kind of PR even if you tried!"

Cally's smile evaporated. "You mean, the reason people are going to be interested in my fashion show is because I *killed* someone?"

"Not just 'someone,' darling! It's like you got rid of that Al-Qaeda fellow the clots are so upset about! Of *course* people are going to want to come and see you, Cally! You're a hero!"

"But I'm *not* a hero," Cally protested. "I'm just me. I mean—I want them to like my designs for what they are, not what I've *done*."

"And they *will*, my sweet!" Sister Midnight said, draping an arm around Cally's shoulders. "Curiosity will bring them in, but once they're here, they'll fall in love with your work, just as I have."

"You really think so, Sister Midnight?"

"Darling, I *know* so," she said reassuringly. "And call me Sis."

"I can't believe what just happened!" Melinda shook her head in amazement. "Sister Midnight—*the* Sister Midnight—just offered to host your first collection!"

"Yeah, I can't believe it, either," Cally replied, a dazed look on her face.

"I can't wait to tell Bella and Bette!"

"No!" Cally begged. "Please don't."

Melinda frowned. "Why wouldn't you want everyone to know about something as cool as this?"

"I want them to know, but not right now, that's all. It's just that I'm afraid some of the girls at school might try and screw it up for me."

"You mean Lilith." Melinda sighed. "Okay, I promise I'll keep it on the down low, but you've *got* to give me something in return. How about making me one of the runway models? *Pleeease?*"

"I don't see why not." Cally smiled. "I'll talk to Sis about it."

"*Yay!*" Melinda clapped in delight. "I'm buying something to celebrate! Come with me?"

"Thanks, but I'm going to head back to the Plaza. I need to unpack my sewing machine ASAP if I'm gonna have that many looks ready in two weeks."

Melinda grabbed her friend's hands and kissed the air beside her cheek. "Congratulations, Cally! I'm so happy for you!"

"Thanks for coming with me, Melly," Cally said. "It really meant a lot."

"No problem—see you at school!" With that, Melinda hurried off in search of the ever-elusive perfect shoe, platinum credit card in hand.

As Cally entered the elevator, someone tapped her on the shoulder. Thinking it was Melinda, she said, "What's the matter? Don't they have any slingbacks that fit you?"

"Probably not," Lucky Maledetto replied with a smile.

"What are *you* doing here?" Cally exclaimed.

"You needn't look so surprised to see me! Sister Midnight *does* have a men's department, you know." He chuckled, holding up a small glossy black shopping bag. "I needed a few ties."

"I'm glad to see you," Cally admitted.

"You are?" Lucky's smile grew even wider.

"Yes, I wanted to thank you for the other night. I had a great time before, uh, you know. I'm glad to see you're okay."

"Same here. But aren't you pretty far from home? Do you need a ride back to Williamsburg?"

"No, that's not necessary," Cally said, her smile faltering. "I'm living with my father at the Plaza now."

"Really?" Lucky cocked an eyebrow in surprise. "The Upper East Side is a big step up from Williamsburg."

"Tell me about it!" She laughed, rolling her eyes.

As the elevator doors opened, Lucky reached out and caught her by the elbow before she could step out into the lobby. "Hey—have you been to Central Park yet?"

"I know it sounds dumb, but I guess when you're a native New Yorker, you just don't think of going to touristy places like that," Cally admitted.

"I bet you've never been to the Statue of Liberty, either."

"Guilty as charged."

"That's okay—I've never been to the top of the Empire State Building. Look, we could stand around and compare all the places we've never been to or I can show you around the park. Which would you prefer?"

"I'd love to! See the park, that is," Cally replied.

"There's only one way to do the park after dark," Lucky said, wrapping her hand around his arm. "Come with me—we're going to go see a man about a horse."

Cally leaned back, staring up at the night sky as the horse-drawn carriage slowly made its way through the park, its hooves clopping rhythmically on the black pavement.

"Thanks for suggesting this, Lucky. I can't believe I waited so long to come here." She sighed. "This place is amazing!"

"I know what you mean," he replied. "Nowhere else in the city can you lose all sense of where you are. If you go far enough inside the park, you can't even hear the traffic or see the skyscrapers. It's like you're in your own world, thousands of miles away from your normal life."

Cally turned to look at him for a long moment, studying his profile against the glow of the old-fashioned streetlights that lined the pathways. "Can I ask you something, Lucky?"

"Sure. Go ahead and shoot," he said, flashing her a crooked smile.

"Why are Victor Todd and your dad enemies?"

Lucky shook his head. "Why do you want to know something like that? Besides, what difference does it make?"

"Because Vinnie is your dad and Victor is . . . Victor is my father's liege lord. I mean, by rights, we shouldn't even be *talking* to each other."

"Well, if you really want to know, the truth is that Todd and my dad weren't always enemies. Fact is, they used to be friends."

"They were friends?" Cally frowned. "When was this?"

"Nearly a century ago. Like a lot of vampires, Todd immigrated to New York City in 1918. World War I and the Russian Revolution chased him out of Europe and into America. He came to the city looking for a new start. He and my dad hit it off, and Todd ended up running a string of speakeasies. He was pretty damn good at it, too. He was a top earner for the Strega.

"Then, about fifty years ago, Todd gets the idea for HemoGlobe. It's basically the same thing as the speakeasies, except instead of peddling laced product out of a club, he's delivering it straight or laced right to your door for a monthly fee, just like the milkman.

"My old man was hopping mad when he found out what Todd was up to. As he saw it, legit blood banking cut into his business. And since Todd got the idea for HemoGlobe from working the speakeasies, he figured Vic owed him a taste. But that's not how Todd saw it, of course. So one thing led to another, bada-bing bada-boom, the next thing you know, it's a matter of honor and they're enemies."

"How do you feel about him? Todd, I mean."

"Me? I got no grudge against Vic," Lucky said with a shrug. "I can't fault a guy for seeing a market and taking advantage of the situation. But still, family is family. You got to stick by them, no matter whether it makes sense to you or not. You know how it is."

"Yeah, I'm afraid I do." Cally sighed, snuggling closer against Lucky as he slid a strong, comforting arm around her shoulders.

CHAPTER 8

"Is it okay if I sit here?" Carmen asked, standing at the foot of the table where Lilith regularly held court during the midnight meal.

"Let's see . . ." Lilith looked up from her conversation with Armida Aitken and tapped her chin in an exaggerated display of thoughtfulness. "You were fooling around behind my back with Jules for *how* long? Two? Three months? And now you want to know if it's 'okay' for you to sit at my table? Hmm. Let me think about that for a second. . . ." She paused for a second before flashing her fangs at the redhead. "The answer's *no*! Go find your own table, slut!"

Dejected, Carmen turned away, and the other vamps at the table—all her former friends—started talking. Carmen knew that they were saying mean things about her clothes, hair, and makeup, because that was what she would do if she was in their place.

As nervous as a foot soldier stranded in the middle of a minefield, she glanced around at the other tables in the Bathory cafeteria. Throughout her academic career, she had always been among the anointed, those deemed "popular." But now she found herself adrift in the most hostile territory imaginable—an all-girl prep school.

Despite her constant attempts to imitate Lilith, even going so far as to sleep with her boyfriend, Carmen simply wasn't an alpha type. She didn't have what it took to draw others into her sphere. She wasn't designed for striking out on her own. In fact, the very thought of being without a clique filled her with terror.

The question she found herself faced with was, which faction could she attach herself to now that she had been cast out of Lilith's inner circle? Or, more to the point, which one would be willing to accept *her*?

The natural choice was to try and find a way into Cally's clique, which was quickly evolving into a real contender in terms of popularity. After all, she and Melinda had once been close friends, and Melly was Cally's second in command.

But then again, Melinda was the one who told Lilith about her involvement with Jules. Carmen had too much pride to go crawling to the person responsible for her downfall. Besides, there was a very good chance Cally and the Maledetto twins had not forgotten all the mean things she'd said and done to them while she was riding high.

That left two groups for her to try and work her way into: the Amazons and the Spods. And since she was nowhere jock enough to fit in with the Amazons . . .

"Uh . . . is it okay if I sit here?"

Annabelle Usher looked up from her bag of O poz to stare at Carmen. Although she was one of the brightest students on the rolls, Annabelle's ragged bangs, poorly applied makeup, and badly laundered school uniform made her a frequent target of ridicule—especially Lilith's.

Annabelle studied Carmen for a moment and then glanced at the other girls gathered around the spod table, all of whom, like herself, had suffered at one time or another from Carmen's acid tongue and catty remarks. "What's in it for us?" she asked flatly. "What will you give us in exchange for letting you sit at our table?"

Carmen blinked in surprise. "You actually expect me to *pay* you to sit down?"

"Hey, *you're* the one who asked," Annabelle said with a shrug. "If you don't like it, go somewhere else."

"I've got an iPod!" Carmen replied, hastily pulling the device from her blazer pocket. "It's got a touch screen and can hold over seven thousand songs!"

"Let me see," Annabelle said, snatching up the offered gadget. She contemplated the digital goody for a moment and then slid it into her own pocket. "Okay. I guess that's good enough. For now." She nodded to the empty chair at the end of the table. "You can sit down."

Carmen heaved a sigh of relief. Although it was a serious step down from the Vamps to the Spods, at least she wasn't sitting by herself. Without the chatter of others to distract her, she would have been forced to think.

"And that concludes our class for tonight," Madame Mulciber said to her Basic Alchemy class. "You are all free to leave—oh, except for you, Miss Todd. I would like to see you after class."

Frowning, Lilith returned to her seat. Earlier that evening the class had been given a pop quiz. She was worried that she had failed the quiz. If so, it meant academic suspension for sure.

After the last of the students left, Madame Mulciber motioned for Lilith to approach her desk. The teacher was tall and willowy with a tangled mane of flyaway hair as red as the flames that constantly burned under the huge copper alembic in the corner of the classroom.

"Given your precarious situation, Miss Todd, I took the liberty of grading your paper first," the alchemy teacher said. "Congratulations: you passed."

"You're joking, right?" Lilith gasped in disbelief. "I got an A?"

"I didn't say that—I said you *passed*," Madame Mulciber replied. "I knew you could do better if you simply applied yourself. So, in light of you showing such dramatic improvement in such a short time, I will recommend to the headmistress that you be removed from academic probation."

"So I'm not going to flunk out of school?"

"That's correct." Madame Mulciber smiled. "I feel it's the least I can do. Your mother, Irina, and I were schoolgirls together in St. Petersburg, back when Tsar Alexander II was in power. Tell me, does your father plan to hold your mother's totentanz in America or the Old Country?"

As Madame Mulciber gazed at her, politely awaiting an answer, it suddenly occurred to Lilith that she didn't have the slightest clue what her father was planning.

"He was still working out the logistics when I left for school," Lilith lied as she quickly jotted down some numbers on a piece of parchment, which she handed to her instructor. "Here's my father's *private* cell phone number. Why don't you call him and explain who you are and see if the location for the totentanz has been finalized yet? Oh, and while you're at it, could you tell him I've been taken off academic probation? I'm sure he'll be *thrilled* to hear the news."

CHAPTER 9

Lilith could barely contain her glee as she hurried up the steps of the Belfry, cutting ahead of the line of bridge-and-tunnel wannabes. She had made a brief stop after school to change out of her uniform and into a D&G magenta and black satin tank dress and strappy slingbacks.

"Welcome back, Miss Lilith," the bouncer said, moving to let her pass.

Lilith made her way across the crowded dance floor, reveling in the music pouring from the gigantic speakers that sounded like the heartbeat of some mythic, hard-partying giant.

As she started up the stairs to the converted choir loft that served as the VIP room, Lilith was surprised to see Sister Midnight making her way back down.

"Lilith! Is that *you*, darling?" the businesswoman exclaimed.

"Sis! How lovely to see you again!" Lilith replied, ritually kissing the air beside the older woman's cheeks.

"It's funny we should run into each other like this! I was just thinking about you. I'm planning a fashion show, and I'm looking for some young, popular girls your age to serve as runway models."

"Really?"

"You're the *perfect* example of the market we're trying to reach! I mean, who *wouldn't* want to be you, darling? Are you interested?"

"Of course!"

"Wonderful! I'll have my secretary get in touch with you later and fill you in on the details. It's going to be *the* event of the season—I'm going to make sure everyone who is someone will be there. I promise it will be golden, my dear, positively *golden*!"

Lilith hurried up the stairs to the VIP room, eager to tell the others about modeling clothes for Sister Midnight. The prospect of being the center of attention again was enough to make her giddy. Although she was forbidden to brag about her brief career as the fashion model "Lili Graves," this was completely different. However, her elation collapsed the moment she saw Carmen sitting on the divan next to Oliver Drake, who was talking to Jules.

Carmen glanced up at Lilith and went paler than usual. She got to her feet and headed for the bar, leaving Oliver on his own. Jules, noticing Carmen's exodus, turned to see what triggered such an abrupt retreat.

"Lilith! What a surprise!" He smiled, standing up so he could position himself between the two ex-friends. "We thought you were still grounded."

"My grades improved, so I'm not on academic probation anymore. But never mind that. I want to know what's *she's* doing here," Lilith demanded, pointing at Carmen.

"Well, you haven't been around lately, Lili. . . ."

"So, when the cat's away, the redheaded rat sneaks out and parties with the cat's friends, is that it?" Lilith said hotly.

"We've already gone over this, Lilith," Jules said testily. "The thing with Carmen is over and done with, okay? If you can't handle what went on between us, it's *your* problem, not mine. The only reason Carmen's hanging out here is because Ollie is my friend. I'm not going to snub him just because you're pissed off at his girl." Apparently satisfied everything was settled as far as he was concerned, Jules opted to change the topic of conversation. "So, I guess this means you won't be hanging out with Exo anymore?"

"I wouldn't say that."

Jules's smile was replaced by a scowl. "You're no longer in danger of being kicked out of school. Why would you *want* to keep seeing him?"

"I'm working on a special project with him for extra credit, that's all," Lilith replied with a toss of her head. "Besides, what difference does that make to *you*?"

"I don't like the idea of him spending all that time alone with you, that's all."

"Why? Are you afraid he'll slip me a love potion and steal me away?" Lilith started to laugh, only to halt upon catching the look in Jules's eye. "I don't believe it!" she marveled. "You *are* afraid he'll seduce me!"

"I didn't say that," Jules said sullenly.

"You didn't have to! If you'll excuse me, I would like to have a drink."

Lilith headed over to the bar, silently fuming over Jules's cavalier attitude toward their relationship. The bastard fooled around with her best friend (well, all right, her *closest* friend), got caught at it, and then had the audacity to be jealous of her spending time with his spoddy cousin simply because she was trying to keep from being thrown out of school! Where did he get off being such a hypocritical jerk? He was starting to sound and act more and more like that dickhead father of his. What really pissed her off, though, was the fact that he acted like she had no choice but to put up with it.

"The usual, please," she told the bartender, who handed her a glass of AB neg laced with bourbon. Instead of sipping the drink, she knocked it back like a shot. "Hit me again," she said, rapping the bar with her empty glass. She was pondering her next move when she heard a cry of girlish delight from behind her.

"*You're back!*" Sebastian threw his arms around her in a fierce bear hug. The club promoter for the Belfry was dressed in his trademark platform heels, this time while tricked out in a tight-fitting black Lurex jumpsuit.

"Did you miss me, Seb?" Lilith asked.

"I was heartbroken," Sebastian assured her as he clambered up onto the bar stool beside her. "Absolutely *inconsolable*."

"I missed you, too," Lilith replied, air-kissing his cheek.

"I thought Daddy Dearest grounded you," Sebastian said. "At least, that's what your BFF Carmen told everyone."

"BFF?" Lilith spat. "Parasitic, slutty, loudmouth, hideous, redheaded harpy is more like it."

"*Mee-yow*, darling!" Sebastian chuckled. "Why don't you tell us what you *really* think?"

"It's bad enough I still have to deal with Carmen at school, but having her hanging around at the club is adding insult to injury!" Lilith scowled. "Did you know she's down to taking her meals in the cafeteria with the spods?"

"By the Founders!" Sebastian gasped. "Well, knowing *you*, sweetie, I'm sure you'll figure out some way to get rid of her. I simply must go! Ta!"

Alone once more, Lilith stared down at her empty glass. The night was definitely not going as she had planned. In her mind's eye she had envisioned everyone in the club stopping and applauding her triumphant return to the fold—oh, yes, and Carmen was certainly not included. But the reality was proving far more awkward than awesome.

It was clear Jules valued his friendship with Oliver more than his relationship with her, but not so highly that he wouldn't bang Carmen behind his buddy's back, given half a chance. If Jules was telling the truth and the only reason Carmen was hanging around was because he was still tight with Ollie . . .

"It's good to see you back out on the town again," Oliver Drake said as he stepped up to the bar alongside Lilith. Although good-looking, with a mop of dishwater-blond hair and slate-gray eyes, Oliver was considerably shorter than either Jules or Sergei, with a temper to match.

As Oliver waited for the bartender to serve him his rum and blood, Lilith leaned forward and placed her hand on his arm. "I *really* have to admire your self-confidence, Ollie. Most guys would feel pretty insecure given your situation, but you're pretty cool about it."

Oliver turned to her, a baffled look on his face. "What situation?"

"You know," Lilith said chidingly. "About Carmen and Jules."

Oliver's eyes widened in surprise. *"What?"*

"Oh. I'm *so* sorry!" Lilith said, feigning embarrassment. "I thought you *knew*. I mean, everyone at school knows. . . . I just assumed *you* did, too. . . ."

"That no-good, lying, worthless . . ." Oliver's eyes grew as dark as thunderheads, while his hands curled into fists.

Jules and Sergei were talking to each other while Carmen stood nearby, staring up at a music video playing on one of the flat screens. They had their backs to Oliver, so they didn't see him barreling toward them. Lilith smiled and licked her lips. She couldn't wait to see the look on Jules's face when Oliver sucker-punched him. However, to her dismay, Oliver made a beeline to Carmen, ignoring Jules altogether.

"You! How *dare* you embarrass me like that in front of everyone! You *whore*!" Oliver shouted, slapping the redhead so hard she fell to the floor. Carmen cowered as Oliver loomed over her, the veins in his temples and neck standing out in stark relief. "Everybody's laughing at me behind my back! Is *that* what you wanted? Is that why you couldn't keep your fucking hands off my friends?" he shouted, stabbing a finger at Jules.

Oliver looked down at Carmen, cowering at his feet like a whipped dog. His anger toward Carmen had nothing to do with feeling betrayed by someone he cared for: the redhead was just a convenient sex partner and a means of attracting free-range humans. He never had any plans of binding his bloodline to hers and, to be honest, her constant prattle about Lilith, high fashion, and makeup wore on his nerves. Still, even though he didn't want Carmen, he didn't want anyone *else* to have her, either.

Carmen sobbed, cringing in anticipation of another blow. She looked over at Jules in the hope he would intervene, but instead he looked away, as if what was happening had nothing to do with him. To her surprise, Sergei stepped forward.

"That's *enough*, Ollie!"

"Butt out, Savanovic!" Oliver snarled. "This doesn't concern you!" He tried to maneuver around Sergei, only to have his schoolmate push him back.

"I *said* that's enough!" Sergei repeated, baring his fangs.

Oliver stepped back, looking around uneasily. Everyone had stopped their partying and was staring at him. While there were a few clots hanging around, most of the onlookers were vampires, who knew that for him to publicly take up Sergei's challenge meant more than a drunken fistfight behind the Dumpster in the alley.

"You want her so much?" Oliver sneered, trying to look brave while still backing down. "You can *have* her."

As Sergei bent to help Carmen to her feet, Sebastian arrived, dragging one of the club's hulking bouncers behind him. "I don't care *who* started *what* first," the club promoter said heatedly. "Either kiss and make up or take it outside!"

"Screw this bullshit," Oliver spat, pushing his way past Sebastian. "I'm outta here."

Sergei turned to Carmen. "Are you okay?" he asked.

"Yeah, I guess so." The bruise on her cheek where Oliver had struck her was already starting to fade like breath on a windowpane.

"C'mon—let's get you a drink." Sergei slid a protective arm around Carmen's shoulders as he steered her in the direction of the bar.

"Are you happy now?" Jules asked Lilith sourly. "Did you get it out of your system?"

"Not entirely." Lilith scowled, displeased by the unexpected turn of events. When she came up with the plan, she hadn't taken Oliver being chickenshit into account. Now, instead of banishing Carmen from their social circle by destroying the friendship between Oliver and Jules, Lilith's scheme had hooked Carmen up with Sergei, Jules's best friend.

As she sipped her latest drink—was it her fourth? Fifth? She'd lost count along the way—she noticed a tall figure in a navy pea jacket, a black wool watch cap pulled low over his forehead, making his way through the crowd of partygoers. When she recognized him, her pulse suddenly raced.

"Oh! Look who's here!" Lilith said excitedly, bouncing up and down on the soles of her feet as she waved her hand in the air. *"Yoo-hoo—Exo! Over here!"*

"Hi, Lilith. Hi, Jules," Xander said. His eyes locked on to her as if she were the only girl in the room.

"What are *you* doing here?" Jules demanded, flabbergasted by the sight of his cousin in such a public place. Although he was nowhere near as monstrous in appearance as his father, Xander's peculiarly long fingers and milk-pale skin did nothing to help him blend in with the locals, even in a vampire-friendly nightclub like the Belfry.

"Lilith asked me to come by," Xander explained.

"She did, did she?" Jules said, turning to glare at his girlfriend. "Why would she do *that*, I wonder?"

"I thought it was only *fair* to invite him, darling,"

Lilith said blithely, ignoring the dark look on Jules's face. "After all, he *is* the one who helped me pass Basic Alchemy! I wouldn't be here partying at all if it wasn't for dear Exo!" She turned and smiled at Xander. "You prefer O neg, am I right?"

Jules waited until Lilith was safely out of earshot before turning to glower at his cousin. "She knows your type?"

"What's so weird about that?" Xander said defensively.

"It's about as weird as Lilith inviting you out to the club in the first place!" Jules retorted. "What's going on between you two? What are you trying to pull?"

"I've simply been tutoring Lilith so she can pass her alchemy class, that's all," Xander replied, clearly stung by his cousin's accusation. "You know, maybe if you actually paid some *real* attention to her and made her feel good about herself instead of cheating on her all the time, you wouldn't feel so damn insecure about Lilith and me being friends!"

"Right! Like *I'm* going to take relationship tips from an Orlock!" Jules snorted, rolling his eyes. "What do you know about having a girlfriend, bat boy?"

"Oh, yeah?" Xander replied. "Well, we Orlocks might not be much to look at, but at least we can *read* above a third-grade level!"

"Shut up, Exo!" Jules snapped, his eyes flashing genuine anger.

"Did you say Jules can't read?"

Lilith had returned from the bar, drinks in hand, and was staring at the bickering cousins, her mouth hanging open in amazement. The look in her eyes was enough to make the pit of Jules's stomach drop away.

Xander nodded. "I do *all* his homework assignments, and he simply recopies them in his own hand. He's barely able to read and write."

"That's not true!" Jules protested. "I *can* read!"

"Yeah, in *English*," Xander retorted. "When it comes to chthonic script, he's functionally illiterate. He's barely able to sign his name."

"I said shut up!" Jules shouted, lunging at his cousin, fangs bared.

Xander moved so fast Lilith didn't see it. One minute he was standing there, the next his over-long fingers were wrapped tightly about Jules's throat. His cousin's feet dangled inches above the floor.

"You might have been able to get the best of me in the nursery," Xander growled, his blue eyes burning with a strange inner fire as he watched his attacker struggle in vain to break free of his grip. "But we're not kids anymore, Jules! I'm tired of being the de Laval whipping boy. I don't like it coming from your father, and I *despise* it coming from you!"

"Sweet hell! What is *wrong* with you kids tonight?" Sebastian cursed, pushing his way through the crowd of onlookers. "Can't you party for fifteen minutes without trying to kill each other?"

Xander let Jules drop to the floor like a bag of wet cement. As he watched his cousin and oldest friend gasp for air, the blue fire in his eyes died and was replaced by self-disgust.

"Jules! I'm *so* sorry!" he said, moving to help his kinsman to his feet. "I don't know what came over me—I swear I didn't mean to hurt you."

"Don't touch me!" Jules snarled, slapping away Xander's hand.

Suddenly aware of the eyes focused on him, Xander hurriedly left the converted choir loft, a pained expression on his face. As he shouldered his way through the packed dance floor toward the exit, one of the drunken partygoers grabbed his forearm.

"Hey, buddy! Who do you think you are? Pushin' people around like that?" The drunk's eyes widened in amazement when he saw Xander's mouth. "Holy shit— what's wrong with your teeth?"

Xander jerked himself free of the human's grasp and, covering his fangs with one hand, fled the club.

"I can't believe he would do something like that to me!" Jules wheezed in stunned disbelief.

"You *did* attack him first," Sergei pointed out.

Lilith shook her head in disgust. "I've had it with you, Jules! I've put up with you cheating on me with my friends and sneaking around with the Monture girl and embarrassing me in front of everyone. But I will *not* tolerate weak blood! And neither will my father!"

"Lili, wait! Don't go!" Jules begged, grabbing her by the hand. "What Xander said isn't true!"

"Let go of me!" Lilith snapped, jerking free of his grasp. "It's *over* between us, Jules! I mean it this time!"

Jules watched as Lilith stormed out of the club. Over the course of their lengthy promisement she had threatened to break things off once and for all on more than one occasion, but now, for the first time, he was afraid she genuinely meant it. Saying he had weak blood was like a curse. As he wondered what to do, there was a timid tap on his shoulder. He turned to find Carmen standing next to him, a hopeful look in her eyes.

"Are you okay?"

He didn't reply but instead shrugged the redhead off like a badly fitting coat. Carmen gazed after Jules as he walked away, hoping against hope that he might stop and turn to motion for her to join him. But he kept on walking without a backward glance. As she watched him go, the last tiny flame Carmen had kept kindled in her heart for Jules guttered and died.

"Can I see you home?"

Sergei wasn't an Adonis like Jules, but he was certainly handsome, in a dark, boho poet kind of way. Sure, he was a total dog, but at least he was honest about it. And he at least seemed to *want* to be with her. In the end, it was all about not being alone, wasn't it?

"Sure," Carmen said with a shrug. "Why not?"

Lilith was on her way to her bedroom on the second floor of her family's penthouse when her father stepped out of the shadows at the head of the stairs.

"What in the name of the Founders is wrong with you?" Victor Todd barked. "I permit you to go out and spend time with your friends only to end up receiving an irate phone call from Count de Laval *screaming* in my ear about you publicly humiliating his son! Lilith, did you break your promise to Jules in front of an entire *nightclub*?"

"Oh—that," Lilith said with a shrug. Her head was swimming from so much alcohol, she had to grip the banister to keep herself upright.

"By the Darkest Powers! Have you lost your mind, Lilith?" Victor asked, clearly exasperated. "You know perfectly well since Jules is of aristocratic blood, only *his* side of the family has the power to break the marriage contract. And even if you *did* have that power, you certainly don't do it in front of a group of drunken ne'er-do-wells!"

"Why should I care if Jules's precious little ego is crushed in the presence of an audience?" Lilith replied defiantly. "He doesn't seem to care that he's humiliated *me* in front of everyone I know. If you ask me, he can dish it out, but he can't take it, the big crybaby."

"You're the one acting like a selfish, spoiled child!" Victor retorted. "It doesn't seem to matter to you in the least that your poor mother and I worked hard to arrange this union with the de Lavals! Do you think you can just stroll off and find yourself another noble of Jules's rank and potential? We're lucky the de Lavals are still willing to go through with the marriage now that your mother's bloodright is no longer part of the dowry. Now you go ahead and do something as foolish as *this*? Over what? A silly affair with your best friend?"

"Carmen's *not* my best friend!" Lilith slurred. "Why do people keep calling her that?"

The tycoon shook his head in confusion. "I don't understand fledglings today. When I was your age, things weren't this complicated."

"When *you* were *my* age, Beethoven was rocking the charts," Lilith sneered.

"My point exactly! Your generation has been brainwashed by the clots and their culture! It's always been a threat to our people, but now it's so *pervasive*, so *instantaneous*—it's impossible to keep our children from being corrupted! I'll admit, sometimes I am sorely tempted to side with Mauvais and his Purist claptrap! Honestly, Lilith—to expect Jules to act like a *human* boyfriend is ridiculous!

"It's in his DNA to be with as many females, vampire and otherwise, as he can possibly manage. After all, our entire race sprang from just *thirteen* males! Monogamy is not a natural instinct among the males of our species. That's something you simply have to learn to accept. At least take some comfort in knowing his bloodright is yours and no other's. That's the best you can expect from your mate."

"Ha! That's rich! *You* complaining about clots being a bad influence! You're the one who had a child by a human mistress! I've got news for you, Dad: my 'poor mother' might have put up with you constantly running around on her, but that doesn't mean *I'm* going to tolerate it!

"Nor am I going to put myself through what she did and suffer decades of miscarriages simply to produce an heir—only to end up incapable of bonding with whichever child finally survives. Times are changing, Daddy dearest. You should know—you helped kick off the social revolution. And FYI: I didn't dump Jules because he was fooling around on me—I did it because he's weak-blooded."

"What?" Victor blinked in surprise. "That's ridiculous! The boy is one of the finest athletes Ruthven's has ever produced!"

"Yeah, but he can't read chthonic script any better than an eight-year-old! He's functionally illiterate. Xander told me so. He's been doing Jules's schoolwork for him for years. It's a pretty good joke, though, don't you think?" She giggled. "What with Count de Laval being *so* obsessed with keeping the Old Blood traditions alive and preserving our culture—and here's his only son and heir, unable to read and write in his own language!"

"Still, that's no excuse for what you did tonight, Lilith," Victor replied sternly. "You're going to get on the phone and call Count de Laval and apologize, right this minute."

"I don't care what you want. I *refuse* to apologize to Jules! You can tell Count de Laval the only way I'll take his son back is if he comes crawling to me on his hands and knees, admitting he was wrong to treat me the way he did. And if you pressure me about this, I swear I'll tell Count de Laval about Cally being my sister. *That* little tidbit of information should be enough to guarantee he'll tear up the contract himself, don't you think?"

"You wouldn't dare!"

"Just try me," Lilith said, looking her father in the

eye. "I don't give a damn about anyone but myself. I guess you could say I'm a chip off the old block. Now, if you'll excuse me, I need to go to bed. Tomorrow *is* a school night, after all."

CHAPTER 10

For the first time in her life Cally had access to any fabric she wanted, not just those she could afford. Although Baron Metzger had offered to buy her a top-of-the-line computerized machine, She insisted on using the same old mechanical Brother sewing machine her grandmother had given her for her twelfth birthday. The Baron had also graciously allowed her to turn the second of his apartment's three bedrooms, the one usually reserved for his son whenever he was in town, into a makeshift studio.

The last week had been something of a blur, what with her time being split between school and putting together several new designs for the upcoming show. She was still two short of her intended goal. Although the pace was grueling and left her little time for anything besides school, she was grateful for the distraction, since it kept her from thinking about her mother and Peter.

She was interrupted while making a delicate cut in some jade shantung by the entrance of Baron Metzger's undead manservant.

"Miss Cally?"

"Yes, Edgar?"

"A Jules de Laval to see you."

"Jules? What are you doing here?" Cally asked as she walked into the living room. She was surprised to find the young nobleman already making himself at home on the sofa.

"I heard you were living in the Plaza with your dad, and I thought I'd pop by and say hello. I haven't seen you since the Grand Ball—what's been happening?"

"I've been . . . busy," Cally said cautiously as she sat down beside him. "To tell you the truth, I'm surprised to see you here. Your father doesn't approve of true-bloods associating with hybrids. He wanted the Synod to declare me a threat to the Blood!"

"I can't help how my dad is," Jules said with a shrug.

"I won't hold you responsible for what your father does, just like I don't blame Melly for anything *her* dad says, but what about you?" Cally asked. "How do you feel about me now that you know I'm half human?"

Jules smiled and leaned forward. "When I first met you, Cally, I realized right then that you weren't like any girl I'd ever known. Maybe the fact that you have human blood explains it. Now that I know the truth about you, I find you even more attractive than before. . . ."

"That's really sweet of you to say, I guess," Cally replied uneasily, removing his roving hand from her knee. "Is that why you came to see me?"

"To be honest, ever since the Grand Ball I haven't been able to get you out of my head." He flashed his trademark smile as he leaned in closer. "I can't forget how you felt in my arms when we danced that night or how your eyes sparkled when you looked at me. . . ." Jules moved in closer, his irises glowing in the dim light of the room like those of an animal. "I keep thinking about the kiss we shared at the club that night . . . how good it felt . . . how *right* it felt. . . ."

Cally could feel Jules's body heat radiating from him, mingling with the musky scent of his cologne. He kept leaning toward her as he spoke, his voice pitched in such a way that it was necessary for her to move in closer in order to hear him clearly. Cally was on the verge of being mesmerized by his voice when she felt his hand traveling too quickly up her thigh.

"I think you'd better go now, Jules," she said sternly, getting to her feet.

"There's no need to look so frightened!" Jules laughed as he stood up. "Are you worried about Lilith? Don't be! We broke up."

"Yeah, I know," Cally replied. "I heard all about it at school."

"Really?" he asked, instantly dropping the smooth seducer act. "What else did you hear?"

"That you and Xander Orlock got into a fight at some club. Look, Jules, I like you. You know that. But I'm not interested in being used like Carmen, understand? I know you only want to be with me because you know it will make Lilith nuts."

"That's just not true!" he protested, caught off guard. "And even if it was, you have no reason to be afraid of Lilith. You don't have to be afraid of *anyone*! You have the Shadow Hand!"

Cally gave Jules a disappointed look. "You just don't get it, do you? I don't *want* this power, and I certainly don't relish it! I never want to use the Shadow Hand ever again. And I certainly don't want to have to use it against Lilith!" Seeing the blank look in Jules's eyes, Cally realized that she had no choice but to go straight to the bottom line with him. "Even if I *didn't* have the Shadow Hand, I still wouldn't want to get involved with you. I'm coming out of an intense relationship that ended very, very badly. It was with someone I never should have fallen in love with, and I'm not ready to put myself back into that kind of situation. I'm sorry, Jules. Really, I am. I'm willing to be your friend, but that's as far as I'll go."

"You mean I'm stuck in the friend zone?" He tried to make a joke of it.

"Afraid so. And because you are, that means you do not get to pass Go, you do not get to collect two hundred dollars, and you definitely do not get to second base."

"Cally—I'm sorry—I didn't mean to come on so strong."

"Well, you *did*," Cally said, pointing to the door. "Please leave now."

The speakeasy was in the subbasement of a trendy, upscale boutique hotel on Sixty-second that catered to Japanese executives visiting the heart of the City That Never Sleeps. With its dim lighting, dark wood paneling, and maroon velvet draperies, it looked like any other cocktail joint in the city, except there was no mirror behind the bar and no liquor to be seen.

"What'll it be?" the bartender asked, barely bothering to look up from the glass he was cleaning.

"B neg and scotch."

"You sure you're old enough, kid?"

"My friend Andrew here can vouch for me," Jules replied, pushing a crisp twenty across the counter.

"Well, if Andy says you're cool, that's fine by me," the bartender said as he palmed the bill. He poured the drink into the glass he'd been cleaning and handed it to Jules.

As he slid into one of the horseshoe booths, Jules tried to figure out where he'd gone wrong. He had smiled, used eye contact, and said all the things girls seemed to want to hear and done it in as nonthreatening a manner as possible. He'd even told her that she was special, and for once it wasn't actually a lie.

So how did he end up sitting by himself at a vampires-only bar instead of rolling between the sheets with Cally Monture? The only other time he'd struck out this badly was with Melinda Mauvais. What went wrong?

He was pretty sure the thing about her ex-boyfriend was just an excuse. If she'd been that into someone else, she wouldn't have been so willing to dance with him at the Viral Room. Maybe Cally's lack of interest had to do with what she'd heard at school. What if Lilith was telling everyone he had weak blood? He certainly wouldn't put it past her, the vindictive little minx.

"My, my, my! If it ain't Little Lord Fauntleroy!"

Jules looked up from his drink to see Lucky Maledetto standing in front of him. Elegantly dressed in a tailored Armani suit, Lucky wore the telltale black silk shirt and crimson Strega tie. Standing next to him was a huge block of undead muscle with fists like sledgehammers and a neck the size of a bull's.

"Oh, hey, Lucky," Jules said, inwardly cursing himself. He should have known better—almost every vampires-only bar in the triborough area belonged to Vinnie Maledetto.

"Mind if I sit down?" Lucky asked as he slid into the booth alongside Jules.

"I guess not. . . ."

The man mountain slid into the other side of the booth. "I guess you won't mind if my bodyguard Bava here joins us?" Lucky said.

"Sure." Jules was trying hard not to look intimidated as he sipped at his drink.

"So, Jules—what brings you to my fine establishment?"

"I just happened to be in the neighborhood and decided to stop by for a drink, that's all."

"Just in the neighborhood, huh? You wouldn't have been visiting our mutual friend, Miss Monture, over at the Plaza, would you?"

"So what if I was?" Jules replied, prickling under Lucky's prodding.

"No need to get testy, Your Highness. I'm just saying, okay? It's a free country, right? People are free to come and *go* as they like. They're even free to disappear, if they keep coming back where they're not welcome.

That's what's great about this country. You get me?"

"Yeah, I got you, Lucky."

"Good. Now get outta here. You're too young to be in this joint, anyways."

"I'm off," Jules said, downing the last of his drink.

"Don't worry about the tab." Lucky smiled, patting Jules on the shoulder as he slid back out of the booth. "The drink's on me. It's the least I can do."

Although he lost interest in Carmen long before Lilith discovered their affair, Jules didn't want to spend any more time alone. Knowing her parents were away, Jules made his way over to Carmen's Park Avenue high-rise. The doorman nodded in welcome, recognizing him from previous visits.

Jules pushed the buzzer on the front door of the Duivel apartment. He knew Carmen was home because he could hear music playing inside. When no one answered, he leaned on the buzzer again. The volume of the music dropped suddenly and he could hear the sound of bare feet on the hardwood floor.

"Who is it?" Carmen asked, her voice muffled by the door.

"It's me. Open up."

There was a lengthy pause before the door finally opened to reveal Sergei Savanovic standing on the threshold, barely wearing his black leather pants. Jules looked past him and saw Carmen sprinting into the kitchen, naked as a baby bat.

"Sorry, dude," Sergei said with an apologetic shrug. "Carmen's busy."

Jules was completely at a loss to understand how, in just a matter of days, he had gone from Mr. Popularity to having no one to hang or party with.

While he was accustomed to Lilith getting mad and dumping him, what he wasn't used to was her staying mad and refusing to take him back. Not only had Cally shot him down, Lucky Maledetto had made it plain that he was better off not trying anything further with her. Now, adding insult to injury, Carmen had not only moved on—she had taken his closest friend with her.

Oh, and he could forget about hanging with Oliver or Xander from now on, too, thanks to Lilith. The other Old Blood girls he could hit on were all Bathory students, so whatever Lilith was saying about him at school, odds were they had heard it, too. What if they *all* knew the truth? What if they *all* laughed in his face and called him stupid? What then?

As he walked down the street, he spotted a couple of young coeds sitting at a patio table outside a nearby bar. They were giggling over their apple martinis while not-so-secretly checking him out. The world was filled with women who found him desirable and would do anything to be with him. He returned their interest with a cocky smile, and they invited him over. In a sudden flash Jules realized his girls didn't need to be Old Bloods—or even vampires, for that matter. If he kept his cool and his distance, Lilith would eventually weaken and come back to him, like she always did. If she thought he was going to beg her to take him back, she had another thing coming.

CHAPTER 11

"I'm sorry I'm late, Sis," Cally said. "Getting set up took longer than planned, but I've got the rest of the collection here, ready to go!" The undead servant accompanying Cally trundled a wheeled garment rack out of the freight elevator as she spoke.

"Perfect!" Sister Midnight fingered the blue suede dress. "My seamstress team will handle the actual fittings once the runway models are selected," she said, motioning to the undead who sat hunched over the sewing stations and cutting tables that filled the huge, open third-floor space. "Tonight you need to decide which models you'll be using and which look each girl should wear. Plus you need to confer with the dressers about the makeup and hairstyle you want for each look. It's *very* important to get all this right. Remember, you only get *one* chance to impress the audience! It doesn't matter how wonderful a particular outfit is if it's being worn by the wrong model."

"I understand, Sis."

"Come with me, then," the older woman said, ushering Cally down a corridor, away from the hum of the sewing machines. "I've set aside part of the loft for an audition. You'll be looking at girls I normally use to model clothes on the shop floor. . . ."

"Are they undead?" Cally asked.

"Sweet hell, no!" Sister Midnight laughed. "My customers would never buy anything modeled by the undead, no matter *how* chic! Undead models lack the necessary *joie de vivre*. Now, where was I? Oh, yes! As I said, most of the models you'll be reviewing are from my usual pool. However, I've called in a few talented amateurs, if you will: younger girls who are leaders in the market we want to reach. I would like to use as many of these girls as possible, if you don't mind."

"Whatever you say," Cally replied. "I trust your judgment on the matter. Speaking of which, I promised my friend who was with me last time that she could be in the show. . . ."

"The one with the exquisite skin?" Sister Midnight was leading Cally into a large room that was empty save for a table and a couple of folding chairs. "She'll be perfect! Just have her show up the day before the show so my seamstresses can fit the ensemble she'll be wearing." Cally sat down at the table as the boutique owner turned to her assistant. "We're ready to start the auditions."

As the assistant opened a door at the far end of the room, Cally asked as calmly as she could, "How many models do I need to pick?"

She didn't want to come across as giggly and geeky to Sister Midnight, but she struggled to keep from bouncing in her seat like an excited third grader.

"With twelve different looks, I recommend selecting ten more girls. The girl you choose to serve as the feature model will do double duty, wearing the first and the last outfits, preferably one casual, the other dressy."

The first model was a tall, thin young woman with long brown hair who moved with the practiced stroll of a runway veteran: head up, eyes front, shoulders thrown back, and her pelvis pushed slightly forward. She put one foot in front of the other as if on a balance beam and walked with a commanding stride, her weight on the balls of her feet, not the heels. As she made her turn in front of the table, Cally smiled and nodded.

"She's good," she said. "We could use her."

"Don't make your mind up *too* quickly," Sister Midnight advised. "You have plenty more to choose from. Next!"

Cally soon discovered that the older woman wasn't exaggerating. Since mature vampires couldn't reflect, there were no mirrors anywhere in the store. In order for customers to get an idea of how something might look on them, a wide selection of "demonstration models" in every possible height, weight, hair color, race, and age was made available. And all of them, from the tallest to the shortest, were as adept at strolling the catwalk as the first girl who had auditioned.

After three hours of watching the same perfect walk down the same imaginary runway, Cally's eyes were about to cross from exhaustion. As the last model, a petite brunette, left the table, Cally turned to Sister Midnight with a quizzical look.

"Is that everyone?"

As if in reply, Lilith Todd breezed into the room, acting as if she were the one holding the audition, not the other way around.

"*You!*" Lilith squawked in disbelief when she saw who was sitting next to Sister Midnight at the table.

"Yeah, me," Cally replied sourly. "And I'm as thrilled as you are."

Sister Midnight's smile dropped from her face. "I see you two already know each other. . . ."

"You could say that," Cally said dryly.

"Forget it!" Lilith said indignantly. "I'd rather march down the catwalk wearing a catcher's mitt and a bandanna than this one's label!"

"Don't give me ideas," Cally said with a crooked smile.

As Lilith turned to leave, Sister Midnight launched into action. "Darling! You *can't* back out now! You're an integral part of this show!"

"Too bad!" Lilith replied hotly. "If I'd known she was involved, I never would have agreed to participate!"

"Very well. If you feel *that* strongly about it, then there's no point in trying to talk you out of it." Sister Midnight sighed dramatically. "It's a shame. Why, I just heard back from Lady Elysia about the show. . . ."

"The Lord Chamberlain's wife is coming?" Lilith gasped.

If Jackie O, Princess Di, and Queen Noor were put into a blender, the result would be Lady Elysia, the most glamorous and aristocratic woman in Old Blood society.

"Why should that matter?" Sister Midnight replied with a shrug. "You said you don't want to be involved in the show."

"I didn't say that, not *exactly*. . . ." Lilith backpedaled.

"So you *do* want to be part of the show?" Sister Midnight prodded.

"I want to look at the clothes first before I make my final decision," Lilith replied, glancing meaningfully at

Cally. "After all, I can't be seen associating myself with something cheap and inferior."

"Very well," Sister Midnight agreed. She motioned for Lilith and Cally to follow her down the hall to the alteration room, filled with workbenches and tailor's dummies already dressed in Cally's designs.

Lilith prowled about, alternately scowling at the outfits on the dummies and glowering at Cally, who was standing next to the door, arms folded.

"Okay. I'll do the show, but under *one* condition: that I walk the runway in *that* dress," Lilith said, pointing to an ethereal, white diaphanous chiffon gown with a sweetheart neckline that was as beautiful as it was simple.

"It's not my call," Sister Midnight explained. "It's up to the designer to decide which model wears what ensemble. Cally? What do you think?"

Cally rolled her eyes in exasperation. Of *course* Lilith would pick that one! It was the best piece in the entire collection!

"I promised my best friend she could—"

Before the words were halfway out of her mouth, Sister Midnight pulled Cally aside. "I realize that this is an awkward situation for you, my dear," she whispered. "Had I known there was, *ahem*, history between you two, I might have made different arrangements. But to be frank, we need Lilith . . . she carries a lot of weight with the crowd I'm looking for. Plus she would look *incredible* in that gown! Still, the decision is up to you."

As much as Cally would have loved to tell Lilith she couldn't be in her show, she realized that would guarantee its doom. Despite her mega-bitch personality or perhaps *because* of it, Lilith was the most popular girl at Bathory Academy and one of the most recognizable faces of the VIP crowd.

Having Lilith involved didn't mean the show would be an automatic success, but having her actively dissing it spelled disaster. Cally knew from personal experience that Lilith would do whatever was in her power to make sure the market Sister Midnight was banking on would stay away in droves.

As Cally watched her demi-sister examine one of the dresses, she knew that in the end, the best way to keep Lilith from sabotaging the show was simply to make sure she was a part of it. Although she was a conniving bitch, there was no way Lilith could pass up a chance to be the center of attention, especially if the audience consisted of super-elite trendsetters.

Besides, she had to admit Sister Midnight was right: Lilith would definitely rock that gown. And in the end, wasn't that what it was all about? Picking the right model for the right outfit, no matter how she might feel about her personally?

"I guess I can put Melinda in the burnt orange. . . ." Cally giggled.

"*Perfect!* It's all settled, then!" Sister Midnight exclaimed with a clap. "Lilith—Cally has decided that you're to be our feature model! That means you will open and close the show! All you have to do is come in the day before the show for your fitting and dresser consultation."

Lilith beamed. "I can't *wait* to tell everyone at school about Lady Elysia!" She already had her iPhone out so she could call her newest crop of friends to inform them of the good news.

"Yes, you do that," Sister Midnight said encouragingly as she escorted Lilith back to the elevator. "Invite *all* your young friends! And tell them to invite all *their* friends as well! It will be the event of the Dark Season!

"Well, we dodged a stake on that one," Sister Midnight said as the elevator doors closed.

"Lady Elysia is really coming to my show?" Cally asked excitedly.

"Of *course* not, dear," Sister Midnight replied matter-of-factly.

"But you told Lilith you heard from Lady Elysia. . . ."

"Yes, that I did," Sister Midnight admitted. "She notified me that she can't come. As for claiming the Lord Chamberlain's wife would be in the audience—I never once said that."

"You sure played to Lilith's ego to get what you wanted out of her." Cally chuckled admiringly.

"I should hope so," Sister Midnight said with a wink. "Vanity is my business."

"You heard me, Armida: Lady freaking Elysia is going to be at *my* fashion show!" Lilith rode the elevator up to her penthouse, cell phone clamped to her ear. "No, I'm *not* the designer! Besides, who the designer is doesn't really matter, anyway! I'm the *feature model*! I'm the *star* of the show! Yes, I *know* it's awesome! You and Lula and the others have *got* to come and be my cheering section! I'll get you seats close to the runway! I'll—I mean, it'll be so cool!"

After she finished talking to Armida, Lilith hit the next speed dial.

"What the—!" she yelped, trying not to drop her iPhone as she nearly tripped over the set of Louis Vuitton luggage parked inside the front door. "Who left this shit sitting here?"

"I did," Victor Todd replied. "I'm leaving this evening for Russia."

"Russia?" Lilith frowned. "Why are you going there?"

"I've got HemoGlobe business in St. Petersburg," Victor said frostily. "As I told you the other day."

"You're not expecting me to go too, are you?" Lilith

asked warily. "There's this fashion show this weekend I've agreed to be in . . ."

"Fashion show?" Victor exclaimed in disbelief. "After that foolishness with the photographer!"

"No, it's not like that—I swear! I didn't have anything to do with this! Sister Midnight asked me to be the feature model for a show at her boutique. *Everyone* is going to be there!"

"Honestly, Lilith, every time I think you couldn't be any more selfish, you still manage to surprise me. Do you think the de Lavals are going to like this?"

"But I'm *not* being selfish!" Lilith protested. "I *am* thinking about family! When Sister Midnight first asked me to be part of the fashion show, I wasn't that interested," she lied. "But when I discovered the designer was Cally, I felt obliged to participate. . . ."

Victor frowned. "Cally's having a fashion show at Sister Midnight's?"

"You didn't know that?" Lilith asked, genuinely surprised.

"No, I didn't," he said uncomfortably. "I've been very busy lately. And Metzger didn't bother to inform me." Victor studied Lilith for a long moment, trying to decide whether he should believe her or not. "Given what you've told me is true, why the sudden change of heart?"

"I realize now, all that's left of the Todd family is you, me, and Cally. She is my sister. I accept that now,"

Lilith said smoothly, but seeing the skepticism in her father's look, she added, "I've decided it's better to have her as an ally than an enemy since she can kill people simply by touching them. Things haven't been that great between us up to now, but I want to change all that. I understand Cally's not supposed to know Baron Metzger isn't her real dad, but that doesn't mean I can't start being a sister to her. I thought by working with her on this project, I could start to make things up to her. . . ."

"Princess, you don't know how much it means to me to hear you say that," Victor said, embracing his daughter. "Very well. You may remain in New York, with my blessings."

As her father hugged her tight, Lilith smiled triumphantly to herself. It was good to know that even after all that had happened lately, she could still wrap her dad around her little finger.

CHAPTER 12

As the sun began to sink behind the towering sky-scrapers, the undead in the service of Sister Midnight awakened from their daylong hibernation and immediately set to work preparing their mistress's place of business for that evening's fashion show. There was much to be done before the doors of the store opened at the witching hour.

The racks and shelves containing merchandise were moved aside to clear a space for the presentation stage and catwalk. The audience seated closest to the catwalk was given padded chairs, while those farther back had to make do with folding chairs set on metal risers.

Draperies were hung from the ceiling to block off the rear of the stage so no one could see the models before they appeared on the catwalk. The sound system was set up and tested for feedback and to make sure the announcer—none other than Sister Midnight herself—could be heard over the music playing in the background.

"There you are, dear!" Sister Midnight exclaimed, hurrying to greet Cally. She was wearing a wireless headset and held another out for Cally. "Put this on immediately! The dressers know to take orders from you if there are any problems backstage."

"What kind of problems?" Cally asked as she put on the headset.

"Broken zippers, late models . . ." Sister Midnight said, beginning a long list of possible disasters. "You know: the usual."

At their best, fashion shows are as perfectly timed as the finest Swiss watches. If everything goes as planned, the models strut down the runway, impressing the audience with their impassive stares, perfectly coiffed hair, and flawless makeup as well as their taste in clothes. Everything is cunningly designed to make it all seem as effortless, simple, and easy as putting on clothes and walking down the street. As if!

Cally already knew that backstage at a fashion show was supposed to be chaotic, but actually being dumped into the middle of it—and being expected to answer questions and solve problems—was something else entirely. Cally made her way behind the curtains to the models' staging area, crowded with clothing racks and makeup tables. The dressers were flittering around their assigned models, adjusting belts, buttons, zippers, and shoe straps like drones in a hive, each in the service of a queen bee.

Cally saw a dresser busily scraping the bottoms of a pair of Prada high heels with a scissors blade so that her model wouldn't slide on the runway. The undead servant didn't so much as glance up as she walked by.

After a little bit of looking, she finally found Melinda, who was being helped into a strapless gown in burnt-orange silk. Mustard-yellow velvet ribbons were sewn across the bodice, and Melinda's dresser was fluffing them out carefully, per Cally's earlier instructions.

"You look wonderful!" Cally said.

"I'm so jittery!" Melinda said as the dresser carefully slid a pearl-studded heel onto her foot. "What if I get out there and fall down?"

"It's a *catwalk*, Melly!" Cally laughed, patting her friend on the shoulder. "What could be more natural for you? Just go out there and wow them with your feline grace!"

"Thanks, Cally." Melinda smiled. "You always know what to say!"

"Places, girls! Places!" Sister Midnight darted back

and forth amid the pandemonium, shouting orders into the headset. "The doors are going to be opening in a few minutes, and I need everyone lined up in order! Cally, make a final pass to make sure everyone looks like they should!"

Cally walked up and down the lineup of impossibly beautiful, perfectly coiffed, immaculately made-up young women dressed in her original creations, making minor adjustments, tweaking collars, and straightening seams as she went.

As she approached the head of the line, she paused. Lilith, dressed in a black silk shift dress decorated with hand-painted abstract flowers, was submitting to the ministrations of her dresser with a passivity Cally would never have imagined possible. It was like watching a fierce bronco meekly surrender to the currycomb of a stable hand.

"I wanted to thank you for agreeing to be a part of the show," Cally said. "It means a lot to Sis—and to me, too."

"Yeah, well—you *did* save my dad's life," Lilith said.

"Cally! Come here!" Sister Midnight called. "Take a look at this turnout!"

Cally gasped as she peeked out at the audience. They were already close to maximum capacity, and the doors to the store had been open for only a few minutes.

Baron Metzger was seated near the front, chatting with a handsome, well-dressed man she didn't recognize. She also saw Bella and Bette flanking a dark-haired woman she assumed was their mother. She looked around, hoping Lucky was there as well, but she didn't see him. She recognized a good number of her fellow students from Bathory Academy, but not in a way that made her feel warm and fuzzy. Sitting close to the runway were Lilith's newest running mates, Armida Aitken and Lula Lumley.

"We must have close to a hundred out there!" Sister Midnight whispered.

"Is that a good thing or a bad thing?" Cally asked uncertainly.

"It's a *very* good thing, my dear! It's a record for this store! And to have this kind of turnout for a new designer is *unheard* of. Some of my customers have come from as far as Paris!"

Cally shook her head in disbelief. Everything was happening so quickly. If someone had told her three months ago that she would be having her very first fashion show in the most prestigious vampires-only boutique in the city, she would have called them crazy. But here she was, doing just that. She only wished her mother and grandmother could be sharing it with her. Then again, they probably wouldn't have been allowed to enter the building.

"Which one of them is Lady Elysia?" Lilith asked. She had left her place in the lineup to sneak a peek at the audience.

"Oh, I'm sorry, Lilith!" Sister Midnight said, feigning regret. "But Lady Elysia can't make it tonight. She called earlier to inform me that something had come up."

"What do you mean, she's not here?" Lilith said angrily. "You *promised* she would be here!"

"I said no such thing," Sister Midnight replied curtly. "However, if you wish to back out of the show, you're free to do so. Otherwise, get back in line until I call your name."

Lilith glanced out at the waiting crowd. As much as she wanted to meet Lady Elysia, that wasn't her only reason for walking the runway. Plain and simple, she needed a fix. She had gotten a taste of what it was like to be a model with Kristof, and she was hungry for more. Grudgingly, she rejoined the lineup.

"Lock and load, ladies!" Sister Midnight grinned. "It's showtime!"

The volume on the techno music blaring from the speakers dropped down to a subsonic throb as the curtains parted and Sister Midnight, dressed in a narrow gold lamé jacket and a pair of black skinny jeans, strode out onto the stage. There was a burst of applause from the audience, which Sister Midnight paused to accept, waving and blowing kisses to her friends. Once the clapping died down, she took her place behind the podium at the foot of the presentation stage and looked out at the assembled spectators.

"Good evening, my friends!" she said, opening her arms wide to embrace the entire room. "And welcome to my humble shop! It is my privilege to introduce to you tonight the maiden collection of a uniquely talented young woman—one already known to most of you, if for a very different reason. I will not say any more about Cally Monture, for I believe the clothes you are about to see speak for themselves. Now, without further ado—ladies and gentlemen, *meine Damen und Herren, mesdames et monsieurs*—I give you the future of fashion!"

The music swelled as Lilith stepped out from backstage and strode toward the catwalk. The moment she set foot on the runway, her fellow students from Bathory jumped to their feet and began applauding and cheering.

Lilith looked out at the hungry, eager faces in the crowd and felt the emptiness within her begin to fill. As the audience focused its attention on her, it didn't see the girl whose mother refused to love her and whose father alternately indulged and ignored her. Instead, it saw a shining, golden girl, a vamp born into immense wealth and privilege who commanded the envy and respect of everyone around her. And when all eyes were focused on her, she truly did feel that she really *was* the icon everyone thought she was. This fleeting glory was infinitely better than the cheap thrills she used to get from peeking at herself in a compact mirror.

As she made her turn at the end of the runway, Lilith felt a tiny spike of fear. Her brief moment in the spotlight was about to be over. She wanted, no, *needed* those eyes trained on her, alternately feeding off her and willing her into existence. She felt that if it didn't continue, she would start collapsing on herself, dwindling away like the Wicked Witch of the West doused with a bucket of water.

As she headed back up the runway, she could see the next model already headed down the catwalk. Lilith was sorely tempted to trip her as they passed each other but held back, knowing it would be a bad move.

"Quick! Get her out of that outfit and into the gown!" Sister Midnight barked.

One of the dressers hurried forward and took Lilith back to the clothing rack where the white chiffon gown awaited her arrival. Lilith allowed herself to be undressed like a giant doll, just like she used to let Esmeralda clothe and groom her when she was a little girl. The attention focused on her by the dresser wasn't nearly as potent as that from the audience, but it would do until she could plug into the real thing yet again.

The second model had finished her walk and was already backstage, and the third girl—a statuesque brunette dressed in a sexy herringbone corset worn with a narrow tweed skirt—was headed for the runway. The fourth model in line, nervously awaiting her cue from Sister Midnight, was Melinda, who was positively stunning. Careful to make sure no one was looking, Lilith stealthily placed her Louboutin on the train of her ex-friend's dress.

"Melinda! Evangeline is making her turn!" Sister Midnight announced. "Get ready to step out!"

Melinda moved forward, only to freeze upon hearing the sound of ripping fabric.

"Oops! I'm *so* sorry, Melly!" Lilith said with an exaggerated look of dismay on her face. "I didn't realize I was standing on your gown!"

"My *ass*, you didn't!" Melinda growled.

"Never mind whose fault it is!" Sister Midnight barked. "Nadja—you're next!" she said, pointing at the model standing behind Melinda. "Someone get some stitches on that gown!"

"That's okay, I'll handle it," Cally said, taking the needle and thread from Melinda's dresser.

"I *knew* that bitch was going to pull some kind of

shit tonight!" Melinda fumed under her breath.

"Hold still, Melly—I don't have time to repair this properly," Cally said as she knelt beside her. "I'll have to baste it and just hope it doesn't show on the runway. As for Lilith: forget her."

"I'm trying." Melinda sniffed. "Really trying."

"There you go!" Cally said, standing back up. "It's not perfect, but it should do until I can fix it later."

"Thanks!" Melinda said, kissing the air beside Cally's cheek. "You're a lifesaver—again!"

"Okay, Melinda—you're next!" Sister Midnight said.

Cally hurried back so she could watch the show and was pleased to hear the chorus of "oohs" and "aahs" that arose from the audience as Melinda appeared on the runway. No one noticed the last-minute repair job, and the dress got the biggest applause of the evening so far.

She glanced over her shoulder at Lilith, who was awaiting her final turn on the catwalk. She wished things could be different between them, but right now if the worst Lilith did was inflict minor wardrobe malfunctions on her fellow models, then Cally took it as a positive sign. Maybe, just maybe, her sister was finally starting to mellow out—if such a thing were possible.

"*Oooooh!* That was so *incredible!*" Melinda exclaimed

as she returned backstage. "Thank you for making that possible!" she said, throwing her arms around Cally's neck.

"You're welcome." Cally laughed. "And you were *amazing*, Melly! I mean it!"

"Lilith—get ready to take your mark!"

"How do I look?" Lilith whispered to Sister Midnight.

"Like the goddess you are," she replied. "Now get out there and walk it like you own it!"

There was a collective gasp of awe from the crowd as Lilith stepped out onto the runway. The applause that arose to greet her as she made her way down the catwalk was almost deafening. The thrill Lilith had gotten the first time was nothing compared to what she was experiencing now. Her heart surged in her chest as if spliced into a high-voltage wire.

Lilith smiled as she turned and headed back to join the other models in a victory lap around the catwalk. Sharing the stage with the other ten models wasn't nearly as satisfying as walking it alone, but it still felt pretty damn good.

Backstage, Sister Midnight turned to Cally and took her by the hand. "It's time for you to meet your public, my dear."

"Not yet—I'm not ready!" Cally protested, hanging back. "I look horrible!"

"Nonsense! You look *fabulous!*" Sister Midnight insisted as she dragged Cally out onto the stage. "See? What did I tell you?" Sister Midnight shouted as the cream of Old Blood society got to their feet, delivering a standing ovation so loud it made the rafters shake. "They *love* you, darling!"

"*Cal-lee! Cal-lee! Cal-lee!*"

Not that long ago, she had been dismissed as a lowly New Blood unworthy of notice, then reviled as a half-human mongrel. Now the exact same people who made every school night living torture were shouting her name and hailing her as a genius. After a lifetime spent pretending she was something she was not, it felt good to finally be accepted for what she was, very good indeed. In fact, the last time she felt this kind of acceptance was from Peter.

The thought of her ex-boyfriend brought with it a melancholy, which she quickly tried to banish. This was not the place or time to feel sad. What was in the past could not be changed. What was done could not be undone, and there was no point in grieving forever—just like Baron Metzger had said. Life was too long for sorrow.

There was a flickering at the corner of her eye, and suddenly Lucky Maledetto was at the front of the crowd, seeming to pop into existence from nowhere, handing her a gigantic bouquet of exotic flowers.

The models headed offstage so they could change back into their street clothes. As she was led away, Lilith paused to shoot a venomous glare in Cally's direction.

Enjoy it while it lasts, sister, she thought. *Because there's not enough spotlight for both of us.*

CHAPTER 13

As Cally stepped down off the stage, Lucky moved toward her, acting as an informal bodyguard as the crowd of well-wishers surged forward. Even though she didn't know most of those in attendance, that didn't keep them from wanting to shake her hand as if they did.

Bella Maledetto pushed past her older brother to throw her arms around Cally's neck. "Everything was so *beautiful*! You really *are* talented, just like Sister Midnight said! I'm so proud to be your friend, Cally!"

"Hey, I was her friend *first*!" protested her sister, Bette.

"Girls! Please!" their mother said sharply, stepping in between the twins. With her classic black silk Dior dress and raven-dark hair pulled into an elegant updo,

Mrs. Maledetto looked like a classical Roman statue brought to life. She addressed Lucky sharply. "Perhaps you would be so kind as to introduce me to your friend, Faustus?"

"Of course, Mama!" Lucky said, giving Cally a sly grin. "Cally, this is my—*our*—mother, Skylla Lamia-Maledetto."

"It's good to make your acquaintance, ma'am."

"My daughters talk of you quite fondly," Mrs. Maledetto said, eyeing Cally as if she were a questionable cut of meat in the butcher's case. "Indeed, *all* my children seem to hold you in high regard, as does my husband."

"I am honored they feel that way about me."

"As well you should," Mrs. Maledetto replied stiffly. "Our family is not free with our friendships."

"Make way!" Baron Metzger called out as he pushed to the front of the line. "Proud father coming through!"

On hearing his voice, Mrs. Maledetto and her brood discreetly faded into the crowd. Cally looked around, but Lucky seemed to have disappeared as quickly as he had appeared. Still, she was relieved the Baron hadn't seen them together.

"Congratulations, my dear! It's a truly marvelous collection!" Metzger said warmly. "By the way—I have someone here who would love to speak with you."

Metzger stepped aside to make way for the man Cally had seen with him before the show started. The stranger looked to be in his early forties, with rust-colored hair and a sharp chin that gave him a foxlike appearance.

"You are the designer?" Metzger's friend spoke with a noticeable French accent.

"Yes, sir."

"My name is Nazaire d'Ombres," he said, offering his hand in greeting. "I am very pleased to meet you, mademoiselle."

"You're *the* Nazaire?" Cally gasped in surprise.

"Mais oui," he said with an impish grin. "Your papa, the Baron, was kind enough to fax me the sketches you made. . . ."

"Oh, monsieur, I'm *so* embarrassed!" Cally said. "I was just fooling around! I hope you didn't think I was being disrespectful."

"Far from it, *ma chérie*!" He chuckled. "In truth, I was most intrigued. I have been in the fashion business a *very* long time. I have had to fake my own death and reinherit my company *twice*! One thing I have learned over the decades is how to recognize talent. You, *ma jolie*, are very talented indeed. And I do not say this simply because your father represents the majority stockholder in my business!

"You possess what it takes to become a great designer.

I know because I have worked with them all—Pierre, Giorgio, Coco, Christian, Karl, Gianni. All of them burned with the same fire when they were young, the fire I see in you.

"I would like to make you a little offer, *m'selle*. Once you graduate from your school, should you still be interested in pursuing a career in fashion, you are more than welcome to come work *pour moi*. It has been some time since Maison d'Ombres last had an infusion of 'fresh blood,' if you will. My label is in need of a younger aesthetic—one you are capable of providing."

Cally's jaw dropped in disbelief. "I—I'm terribly flattered, Monsieur d'Ombres."

"Please! Call me Nazaire!" he said, kissing her hand. "I do not stand on formality with those I consider my friends."

"Monsieur . . . I mean, Nazaire, this is an *incredibly* generous offer you've made. I *really* don't know what to say. I certainly do not consider myself worthy. . . ."

"Nonsense!" he said, dismissing her protests with a wave of his hand. "There's no room for modesty in fashion—false or otherwise! You need not give me an answer now. You are young, and our lives are long. Five months . . . five years, they are the same to us, *n'est-ce pas?*"

* * *

The fashion show was long over, as well as the reception that followed it. Cally sighed in relief as her last fan finally filed out the door of the boutique. It had never occurred to her how exhausting being famous really was.

"You did extremely well for someone who was a complete unknown a week or so ago," Sister Midnight said with a pleased look on her face. "I'm interested in buying the patterns from you. The line will still bear your name, but my seamstresses will be the ones to put everything together. What do you say?"

"I say you have a deal."

"Excellent! I'll have my attorney draw up the necessary paperwork and drop it off at the Plaza for you to sign. Why don't we go up to my office and celebrate with a glass of something good? I have an O neg mixed with Dom Pérignon champagne. . . . "

"You start without me, Sis," Cally called over her shoulder as she ducked backstage. "I'll join you as soon as I double-check to make sure the collection is properly put away."

The staging area that had been a riot of activity a few hours before was now eerily silent. The dressers and models were gone, leaving only racks of clothes and discarded shoes behind as evidence of their existence. As she looked around, she was startled to see the silhouette of a man on the other side of the curtains. She gasped in alarm, her heart leaping into high gear, thinking Peter had succeeded in tracking her down and was about to make her pay for killing his father.

"Who's there?" she called out.

"It's just me—your biggest fan," Lucky said, pushing aside the curtain.

"For a moment I thought you were someone else." Cally sighed in relief. Even though she knew she wasn't in any danger, her heart continued to beat fast.

"Someone you don't want to see, I take it?"

"Never again, if I can help it."

"I wanted to wait until the others left before I gave you this," Lucky explained, fishing a gold necklace from his coat pocket. "I didn't want anyone to get the wrong idea. Or the right one."

"Oh, Lucky!" Cally gasped. "You really shouldn't have! It's beautiful!"

"No, it's not," he said as he helped to fasten it around her neck. "But it will be in a second. Turn around and let me see how you look in it." Cally did as he asked, pirouetting around to face him. Lucky smiled and nodded. "*Now* it's beautiful."

"Thank you, Lucky—I really don't know what else to say! No one has ever given me a present this nice before."

"That'll be changing soon—I'll see to that personally," Lucky promised.

"Where were you keeping yourself during the show? I didn't see you in the audience before it started. Then suddenly—poof! You're right in front of me!"

"I was around the whole time—I was keeping an eye on Mom and the twins. Most people don't see me unless I want them to." Lucky lowered his head and placed the tips of his ring and middle fingers to his brow. The air rippled, like the surface of a pond disturbed by a passing wind, as darkness gathered about Lucky, shrouding him until he resembled a flitting shadow, like those glimpsed out of the corner of the eye.

"Where did you go?" Cally giggled, looking around nervously. "Lucky—?"

Suddenly a pair of strong arms grabbed her from behind around the waist, lifting her off her feet as she was swung around in a circle.

"Boo!" Lucky laughed. *"Gotcha!"*

"No fair sneaking up on me!" Cally squealed in mock protest.

Lucky put her back down but didn't let her go, his hands linked around the small of her back. "You know," he said, looking down into her upturned face. "We never really got the chance to finish our dance that night at the Grand Ball. . . ."

A warning bell at the back of Cally's head began to clang its alarm. The last time she followed her heart, it had resulted in disaster for everyone involved. The safe and sane thing for her to do would be to simply tell Lucky she was flattered but not really interested. It would be a lie, but at least she wouldn't get hurt in the long run. Then she could go join Sister Midnight in her office for that drink and head back home for a well-deserved rest.

She was still trying to figure out the best way to let Lucky down gently when he pulled her close and planted a long, deep kiss on her lips. Instead of pushing herself away, like she told herself she should, Cally melted in his arms, returning his kiss.

When they finally came up for air several minutes later, Cally shook her head in dismay. "We shouldn't be doing this."

"Why not?" Lucky asked, a puzzled look on his face. "You like me, don't you?"

"Yes, I do—very much," she admitted.

"Then what's the problem?"

"The problem is that your father is the sworn enemy of Victor Todd, and my father is . . ." She paused for a second, then quickly looked away. "My father is Todd's loyal vassal. That means, by blood, I am sworn to protect Victor and serve him, as my father has. That makes us enemies. I've lost so much already, Lucky. I don't want to lose you, too."

"It doesn't *have* to be like that," Lucky assured her. "My sisters and I have been discussing things lately and have decided it's time that our father call off his vendetta. We're trying to convince him to do so because of our friendship with you."

"You would do that for *me*?" Cally whispered in amazement. "You would actually make peace between the families?"

"Cally, I would do *anything* for you," Lucky replied, taking her into his arms. "All you ever have to do is ask."

CHAPTER 14

Normally Lilith would have hung around for the reception after the fashion show, but she couldn't stomach having to stand around and watch everyone fawn over Cally. So, while the other models sipped O poz laced with cheap white wine, she changed back into the clothes she arrived in and left. She felt that Sister Midnight had lied to her about Lady Elysia, but she wasn't ready to burn her bridges with the retail tycoon. She had her own ideas that would benefit from her support.

As she rode the elevator down, Lilith recalled the dopey look on Cally's face as she looked out at the crowd gathered at her feet. What an idiot! Did she *really* think everyone genuinely liked her clothes? Didn't she realize that the *only* reason they were toadying up to her was because of the Shadow Hand, not her skill at the sewing machine? They were just there to suck up to her and try to get on her good side so she wouldn't have a reason to kill them later on.

As the doors opened, Lilith was surprised to find Xander standing in the lobby, dressed in his pea jacket and navy watch cap.

"What are *you* doing here, Exo?" Lilith asked as she stepped out of the elevator.

"You sent me a text message asking me to come out and show my support," he said, holding up his cell phone.

You and everyone else on my contact list, Lilith thought. Still, she was secretly pleased that Xander made the effort to show up. She knew his idea of a good time was tinkering with potions, not hobnobbing at fashion shows, so his being there actually meant something.

"Is that a present for me?" she asked, pointing to the black velvet-covered jewelry case he held in his hand. Lilith not only enjoyed receiving gifts from admirers, she more or less expected it. After all, hanging with someone as popular and beautiful as herself was a privilege, not a right.

"Yes, it is," he said, smiling bashfully. "I hope you like it."

"Is it diamonds?" Lilith asked, all but snatching the box from him. "I positively *adore* diamonds." She flipped open the clamshell case and gasped in amazement at the blue diamond tennis bracelet inside, nestled like a tiny, shining snake on a bed of white satin. Lilith lost no time slipping it onto her left wrist.

"I had it commissioned especially for you," Xander explained. "The blue diamonds are the same shade as your eyes."

"Thank you, Exo!" she said breathlessly, admiring her newest trophy.

"Do you like it?" he asked. "Because I can get you something you like better if you don't. . . ."

"Like it?—I *love* it!" she said with a laugh, gently brushing Xander's cheek with the edge of her hand. She was surprised at how good his skin felt against her own. She experienced an unexpected tingle as Xander looked her in the eye.

"If you love that, then you're going to *adore* the other present I have for you."

"Something *better* than a diamond bracelet?" Lilith asked, cocking an eyebrow. "This I've got to see!"

"I was expecting to see Jules at the fashion show," Lilith said as she followed Xander into his workshop. There was a time, not so long ago, when she would have freaked out at the thought of being alone in a room with Exo. Now she found herself psyched while in his company. "Did you see him?"

Xander shook his head. "No, I didn't."

"Have you heard anything from him recently?" Lilith asked as she slid out of her Nanette Lepore coat, draping it over the back of a nearby chair.

"Jules and I haven't talked since that night at the club," Xander reminded her. "The only de Lavals and Orlocks who are close right now are my mother and father. My father and Uncle Julian aren't speaking to each other, either. Hey," he said, changing the subject. "You were a knockout tonight. You were so beautiful in the white dress. You looked like a goddess. I wish I had a picture of you in that gown."

"Yeah, too bad there's no way to photograph me." Lilith sighed. "That way I could look at it and remember what it felt like to walk down the runway. A keepsake, you know? So, where's this gift you promised me?" She loved presents, and Exo had already demonstrated superior taste when it came to jewelry. Lilith rubbed her new bracelet fondly, trying to imagine something better.

Xander knelt beside the chair where she sat so that they were eye to eye and held up a small, unmarked jar. "This is it."

Lilith scowled for a moment, then realization dawned in her eyes. "By the Founders!" she gasped. "Exo! Is that what I *think* it is?"

"There's only one way to find out." He smiled. "Close your eyes."

Lilith shut her eyes, her pulse throbbing in eager anticipation. She flinched as something cold, wet, and sticky made contact with her right cheek. She wrinkled her nose in distaste on catching a rank odor. "Yuck! This stuff reeks of toadstools! I thought you were serious!"

"Hush!" Xander said firmly, continuing to spread the cold goo across Lilith's face. "It smells like that because it has toadstool in it. I'm using the most recent formulation—the one incorporating some of your suggestions, partner. This was *your* idea, after all. We can see about fixing that later. Right now I just need you to stay put and keep your eyes and mouth shut. I don't want to get any of this where it doesn't need to be."

Although she normally disliked being told what to do, Lilith responded to the commanding tone of Exo's voice and the soothing, almost hypnotic sensation of his hands smoothing the cream across her skin.

Xander stepped back to admire his handiwork. "Lilith, you once asked me if you were pretty. I said you were beautiful, but you didn't truly believe me. But now I'm going to prove it to you! I want you to look at me."

Lilith opened her eyes to find Xander pointing a digital camera at her. "Exo—what are you doing?" she gasped. "You know what would happen if anyone saw you with that!"

"Say B neg!" Xander grinned as he snapped her picture.

"*Exo—no!*" Lilith cried out as the flash went off. "What do you think you're doing?"

"Providing you with the confirmation you need," he replied, reversing the camera so that she could look at the display on the back. "See? You *are* the most beautiful woman in the world!"

Lilith gazed in wonderment at the image in the viewfinder for a long moment. The last time she had seen a picture of herself, she had looked like an artsy optical effect, with a body as transparent as window glass. Now she appeared as solid and three-dimensional as any human—except that her hair and eyes seemed to be missing. Jumping to her feet, she fished out a pair of oversized YSL sunglasses from her Prada bag.

"Take another picture!" she said excitedly, sliding on her shades.

This time when Exo showed her the picture, the illusion of normalcy was almost complete. "Too bad about the hair." She sighed. "But I guess I could wear a scarf."

"I'm working on that," Xander said matter-of-factly, pointing to an open notebook sitting on the worktable. "I should be able to bond the active ingredients that allow for reflection into a simple shampoo. And the problem with the eyes can be solved by using contact lenses."

"This is incredible!" Lilith exclaimed in delight. "I can see myself in a photograph! I can actually *see* myself! You're right, this *is* better than a diamond bracelet! Exo, do you realize what this *means*?"

Instead of answering her, Xander pulled Lilith into his arms and kissed her. At first she struggled to free herself from his embrace, but after a couple of seconds she began to respond. To her surprise, Exo was a great kisser—much better than Jules. After a long minute they drew back to stare into each other's eyes.

As she looked up into his face, features she had once made fun of, like his long fingers and pointed ears, no longer repulsed her. In fact, they now seemed to arouse her. She had to admit that Exo possessed a unique aura. Unlike Jules, who was physically perfect no matter which way you looked at him, Xander could look hideously ugly from one angle and then, a second later, somehow manage to appear ruggedly handsome.

The difference between the cousins wasn't limited to physical appearance. Jules's masculinity often seemed to be part facade, whereas Xander's was part of every fiber of his being. Although Xander appeared self-conscious and shy, at his core he was confident in his power and abilities, which Lilith found incredibly sexy.

Wrapping her arms around his neck, she pulled his head back down to hers for a second, lengthier kiss. With Jules, kissing always seemed rushed, as if it was something he had to do in order to get to the next step in his seduction. But with Xander, it was nice and sweet and slow, as if he was trying to savor her instead of devour her. The feel of his full mouth against her own was fantastic, unlike anything she had experienced before.

She moved sinuously against him, like a cat eager to be scratched behind the ears, as his powerful hands traveled over her body. As his long, spidery fingers brushed against the bare flesh of her outer thigh, she arched her spine, tossing back her head as she hissed through her teeth. Xander leaned forward, pushing her against the worktable hard enough to jostle the racks of beakers and flasks.

Lilith boosted herself onto the edge of the table, wrapping her legs around Xander's lower body. As she kissed him, she began to pull his shirt off over his head, running her hands over his totally hairless yet surprisingly broad chest. However, as she began to tug on his belt buckle, Xander abruptly broke free of their kiss and stepped back, gasping like a winded runner.

"Why are you stopping?" Lilith panted, literally trembling with lust.

"This isn't right—we both know that." Xander shook his head. "You're promised to Jules, and despite everything, he's *still* my cousin and oldest friend. I have no right to be with you—especially not like this."

"Jules and I are so over!" Lilith assured him.

Xander's cheeks turned bright red, but he said nothing else as he put his shirt back on.

Lilith quickly hopped down off the table. "Do you *really* think Jules would do the same if the roles were reversed?"

"It doesn't matter to me what Jules would have done," Xander replied solemnly. "It only matters what *I* do. I think you should go home now, Lilith. It will be dawn soon."

As he held the door open for her, Lilith paused to look up at him. "Are you *sure* you want me to leave, Xander?" she whispered, leaning in so close her breasts were brushing against his body.

"We'll talk about this later, okay?" Xander said, letting out a shaky breath. "I think right now—I think we're in danger of letting our excitement get the better of us."

"I certainly hope so," Lilith said.

CHAPTER 15

"**H**ere you go—door-to-door service," Lucky said as his driver pulled up outside the Plaza.

"It's not the first time you've escorted me home," Cally reminded him.

"That's true," he said, leaning in for a long, lingering kiss. After they finished, he smiled down into her eyes, stroking the curve of her cheek with his thumb. "When can I drop by for a proper visit?"

"Give me a couple of nights to break the news, okay?" she replied. "I don't want to be sneaking around behind my father's back. I've had enough of that already."

"I understand," Lucky said. "I'll start in on my dad, too. Don't worry, Cally. We can make this work, baby—I promise you that."

Cally pirouetted her way across the marble lobby of the Plaza, giggling like a schoolgirl in love. The night-shift concierge behind the desk looked up, baffled by such a display of ebullience at six in the morning. Cally's first response was to halt what she was doing and hurry to the elevators, but she stopped herself from doing so. Why should she have to worry about calling attention to herself all the time? After all, why *shouldn't* she giggle and act silly? She *was* a schoolgirl in love!

It had been a fabulous evening—her fashion show was a huge hit, her designs were being picked up by Sister Midnight for sale in her chain of boutiques, she'd been offered an apprenticeship in Paris by none other than Nazaire d'Ombres—and to top it all off, she had a new boyfriend! It would take her hours to come down to earth long enough to sleep. She couldn't wait to tell Baron Metzger everything.

Although he was her father's vassal, she trusted the Baron enough to try to plead her case. Surely Victor would welcome a truce between himself and Vincent Maledetto?

As she unlocked the door to the apartment, it stopped halfway, blocked by something just inside the threshold. She stuck her head into the gap between the jamb and the door, frowning down at the packed suit-cases parked inside the foyer.

"Edgar? What's going on?" she shouted as she squeezed her way inside. "What are my bags doing out here?"

"I do not know, Miss Cally," Baron Metzger's butler said as he stepped into the front hallway, carrying Cally's sewing machine under one arm and a fully loaded steamer trunk under the other. "The master has instructed me to pack your things, so that is what I am doing."

Cally pushed past the undead manservant and hurried in the direction of the living room, where she found Metzger standing in front of the fireplace, drinking blood from a brandy snifter.

"Baron! What's happening? Why are my things sitting in the foyer?"

"I'm afraid I must return to Europe, my dear. Something has arisen that requires my immediate attention. I fear I will be gone for some time."

Cally's heart, which had been as light as spun glass moments before, suddenly transformed into lead. Wonderful! Just as things were really looking up for her, now she was going to be torn away from her friends and opportunities and sent packing to some foreign land.

"Where are we going?"

"I'm afraid you don't understand," Baron Metzger said gently. "You will not be accompanying me, Cally. Where I'm going is very dangerous, even for our kind, and especially for someone your age. Besides, your probationary agreement with the Synod requires that you remain in New York. There is no way you could leave the city without bringing Count de Laval down on you."

Cally frowned. "But if I can't stay here and I can't go with you, where am I supposed to live?"

"Come tomorrow evening, you will be residing with your true father." Baron Metzger smiled, placing his hands on Cally's shoulders. "You will remain under Victor Todd's roof until you have finished your education at Bathory Academy. You have nothing to worry about, my dear. As far as Old Blood society is concerned, Victor is merely extending hospitality to the child of his vassal, nothing more."

A stricken look crossed Cally's face as she realized what Metzger was saying. In the brief time she had spent as the Baron's "daughter," she had become quite fond of the old gentleman. Although her grandfather Cyril had died long before she was born, Baron Metzger treated her the way she always imagined he would have.

"But I don't *want* you to leave, Baron!" she said tearfully, throwing her arms around him, burying her face into his broad chest. "*Please* don't go! Can't you talk my father into letting you stay?"

Metzger gave a deep, sad sigh as he tried to console the weeping girl. "As much as I would like to do so, I must serve the House of Todd as your father sees fit. I have served him without question for over a hundred years, just as I served your grandfather Adolphus before him." He gently disengaged himself from Cally, handing her a linen handkerchief from his breast pocket. "However, I will admit that pretending to be your father has been the most pleasurable task ever commanded of me. I wish you *were* my real daughter, Cally. My beloved wife and I always wanted a little girl, but it was never meant to be."

"Will I ever see you again?" Cally sniffled. All her life she had dreamed of going to live with her real father, but now that she was doing so, she was surprised to find herself ambivalent about the whole thing.

Baron Metzger shrugged. "That depends on the will of your father." He reached out and lifted her chin, holding it with his thumb and forefinger. "Now, now—no crying, *liebchen*. What did I tell you the night your mother died?"

"Life is too long for sorrow," Cally replied, wiping the tears from her eyes.

"That's my girl," Metzger said proudly.

CHAPTER 16

Lilith woke up feeling better than she had in a long time. She hadn't greeted a new evening with such confidence since—well, since before Tanith was killed. And why *shouldn't* she feel on top of the world? Her dream of becoming the most important and powerful vampire in all of history was finally within her grasp.

She was standing on the cusp of being her own woman, finally free of interference from her father and the likes of the de Lavals. From here on in, things were going to be *very* different, not only in her life but in everyone else's as well.

Maybe she would just go ahead and drop out of school. With the kind of money she would be making soon, she could simply hire other vampires to do the things she wasn't good at, such as beastmastery or stormgathering. And if her father didn't approve of her decision to drop out, he could go suck it. Her life was going to truly belong to her now and no one was going to tell her what to do—or *not* do.

As she slid into her cashmere robe, she heard a loud thumping noise coming from the hallway. Lilith opened the door to see one of the maids carrying a large steamer trunk into her mother's old bedroom. She darted across the hall and peered around the doorjamb. A female figure with short, dark hair was standing with her back to the door, removing clothes from an open suitcase sitting atop the bed. Although she couldn't see the woman's face, there was something horribly familiar about the unannounced houseguest.

As Cally Monture turned around to tell the maid where to place the trunk, Lilith's worst fear was confirmed. Tightening the knot on her robe, she ran down the hallway, taking the stairs to the main level two at a time.

Victor Todd was sitting behind his desk, talking on a hands-free headset while working on his computer, when Lilith burst into his office.

"What is *she* doing here?" she demanded angrily.

"Hello, Lilith. Do I not get a 'Welcome back, Daddy—how was Russia?'" Victor said sarcastically, covering the mouthpiece of the headset.

Lilith scowled and rolled her eyes. "Fine. How was Russia?"

"Colder than a polar bear's balls," Victor replied. He took his hand away from the mouthpiece, resuming his conversation. "You heard me—I want someone on this, *fast*! I want to know where it was sent from and I want—no, I *expect*—answers for what happened PDQ! Call me as soon as you get something!" Removing the headset, Victor turned his attention back to Lilith, who was glowering at him, arms folded across her chest. "To answer your first question: Cally is here because Baron Metzger has wearied of playing papa to my cuckoo's egg and returned to Europe. As she is your demi-sister and has no other living family, where else would you have her stay?"

"She could stay at the Y for all I care," Lilith replied, "just as long as it's not here!"

"That's strange," Victor said coldly. "I thought you said you wanted to change things between the two of you. You told me before I left for St. Petersburg that you finally realized the importance of having her as an ally, not an enemy, and that you wanted to be more of a sister to her. Were you telling me the truth when you said that, or were you simply lying to me again?"

"No, I meant what I said," she lied. "But that doesn't mean I want to live under the same roof!"

"Well, that's what you're going to be doing, young lady," Victor replied sternly. "I'm not going to tolerate any more of this Cain-and-Abel bullshit, you understand? The last thing I need is for you to end up like Christopher Van Helsing simply because you provoked Cally into a fight!"

"Okay—but did you *have* to give her Mom's room?" Lilith pouted.

"Why not?" Victor shrugged. "It's not like Irina's going to be using it. Would you prefer I move you into your mother's suite and give Cally your old room?"

"No," Lilith grumbled, dropping her shoulders in resignation.

Victor Todd waited until Lilith was safely out of the office before getting up and locking the door behind her. He had a lot of things that needed to be taken care of now that he was back, and he didn't need any further intrusions.

It was easy enough to explain Cally being brought into the household by claiming the decision was forced on him by Metzger, who Lilith believed was blackmailing him with the pictures the fashion photographer Kristof took when she was posing as the human model Lili Graves.

The truth of the matter was that Victor had grown concerned about the possibility of Cally bonding with his vassal. The girl was in a particularly vulnerable emotional stage, and he did not want Metzger getting any ideas about manipulating Cally's loyalties—and abilities—to his own ends.

After all, whoever held sway over the heart and mind of the one who wielded the Shadow Hand controlled one of the deadliest weapons in this world and the next. But right now he had far more serious matters to worry about than a possible palace coup by Karl Metzger.

Victor sat back down behind his computer and clicked on the toolbar at the bottom of the desktop, reopening the window he closed the second Lilith barged into his office. The LCD flat-screen monitor was filled by the image attached to an anonymously remailed email message with the heading: WE HAVE HER.

The picture was that of a blindfolded Sheila Monture standing before a sheet hung in front of a wall. She looked haggard and frightened but otherwise unharmed. In her hands she held a copy of the *New York Times* with the day's headline and date visible.

Victor sighed sadly as he stared at the mother of his child and, safe in the knowledge that no one could see him, caressed the image of her face with the tip of his finger.

* * *

Cally heard a knock and looked up to see Lilith standing in the open doorway, dressed in a willow-green cashmere robe. It was the first time she had ever seen the other girl without her makeup. She was taken aback at how young and vulnerable Lilith looked au naturel.

"Is it okay if I come in?"

"Yeah, I guess so." Cally shrugged.

Lilith stepped inside, taking in the mahogany rococo bed and other antiques that decorated the room. "So, my dad said you're going to be living here. . . ."

"Yeah, I have to stay here until my father gets back," Cally replied, still waiting for the other shoe to drop.

"Your father? You mean the Baron?"

"Yeah," Cally said, frowning slightly. "Who else?"

"What's that?" Lilith asked, pointing at a bronze urn sitting atop the dresser. "Was that here when you arrived?"

"No," Cally said, quickly putting herself between Lilith and the urn. "Those are my mother's ashes."

Lilith frowned. "I thought humans go into the ground when they die."

"Not all of them," she explained. "Some of them are cremated."

"But why would you want to keep her ashes?"

"So she'll always be a part of my life," Cally said. Lilith stared back at her as if she had answered in Swahili. Cally decided it would be better to change the subject. "There are some clothes hanging in the walk-in closet," she said as she watched Lilith wander around, staring at the furniture and fixtures as if she were in a museum. "Does someone stay here on occasion?"

"This was my mother's room," Lilith replied.

"Oh! I'm sorry!" Cally said, embarrassed. "I had no idea! I just assumed, when you asked me if the urn was here before I arrived, that this was a guest room—"

"That's okay," Lilith said with a shrug. "I've never been in here before. My mom and I didn't talk a lot." She walked back to the door and turned around to face Cally. "You want to go shopping?"

Cally blinked, taken by surprise. "Huh?"

"Not right now, of course," Lilith said, clarifying herself a little further. "But later, once you're unpacked and settled in. We could do Bergdorf's . . . maybe hit a couple of the boutiques?"

"Yeah, that sounds cool, I guess," Cally replied, although she still wasn't sure whether she was walking into a trap or not. "Do you mind if I ask you a question?"

"Sure. Go ahead."

"*Why?*"

Lilith shrugged again. "I hate shopping by myself."

CHAPTER 17

Cally let out a long, slow breath of disbelief. Lilith had actually been *nice* to her. She was tempted to go look out the window and see if there were any pigs flying over Central Park.

Almost as surprising to Cally was the realization she actually felt *sorry* for Lilith. For the first time she had a handle on what drove Lilith to act the way she did. While her own relationship with her mother had been far from perfect, at least she had been secure in the knowledge that Sheila loved her.

Despite Count de Laval and Anton Mauvais's claims, vampires were not that different from their human cousins. They were capable of genuinely nurturing relationships with their offspring, just like any human parent. She had seen it with the Maledetto family, as well as between Melinda and her mother, and even Count Orlock and his grotesquely deformed son, Klaus. She had even experienced it, albeit secondhand, through Baron Metzger.

But to *never* know the security and warmth that came with a mother's love, not because she was an orphan but because her mother *refused* to love her child . . .

No wonder Lilith was such a manipulative, messed-up, chronically insecure bitch.

Perhaps Irina's death had started Lilith seeing things from a new perspective. The sudden loss of someone close had a way of doing that to you, as Cally knew all too well. That might explain her unexpected sea change.

Maybe, just maybe, Cally could finally have a sister in Lilith after all.

Anything was possible.

Lilith left her mother's old room and hurried back across the hall to her suite. She locked the door and threw herself onto the bed, her shoulders shaking as she buried her face into the pillows so no one could hear. After a couple of minutes she finally rolled over onto her back, exhausted by her laughter.

This was going to be so *easy*! Why hadn't she thought of it before?

She had spent so much time and energy trying to best Cally in physical confrontations, only to fail miserably. There was no way she could defeat her in battle: now that she possessed the power of the Shadow Hand, it was too dangerous to continue to blatantly antagonize her.

It was time to change tactics. This time she would take a page out of Carmen's playbook. Instead of treating Cally as her enemy, she would pretend to be her friend and get as close to her prey as possible so she could win her trust. Then she would bide her time until Cally no longer suspected a thing, and, when she wasn't looking—blammo!

Although it galled her to suffer the indignity of sharing a roof with her half-breed sibling, it was only a matter of time before she would be free to call her own shots and move out. When she and Exo finally perfected the anti-vanishing cream, she'd take it to Sister Midnight and show her what it could do. It was that simple. With the proper investors and distributor, they could go international within a matter of weeks. The money would be enormous, as would be the fame and attention.

Lilith's thoughts of worldwide superstardom were interrupted by the sound of something tapping on one of the panes of the French doors that opened onto the small balcony outside her bedroom. She threw back the curtains covering the window, smiling to herself as she saw the pale face pressed against the windowpane, looking into the room with eyes filled with longing.

As she opened the balcony door, she thought about how, after tonight, nothing would *ever* be the same again. Not for her. Not for Exo. And certainly not for Cally. Once customers got their hands on the anti-vanishing cream, it would change the world for vampire and human alike.

Her father's fortunes would seem small compared to the income from the cream. She could do whatever she liked—with whomever she liked. Until then, she would have to bide her time, like a spider in its web, waiting for precisely the right moment to administer the killing stroke.

Just you wait and see, Daddy.